# They Call Me Law 2
## When a Good Girl Meets a  Thug

### By Kelly Marie

© 2016

Published by Leo Sullivan Presents

www.leolsullivan.com

# Chapter One

*Law*

**One month later**

Things had been going very good between Honey and I. We saw each other every day. I spent a few nights here and there at her apartment too. This was all new to me, but I liked it. I had never been one to go by a female's house; I didn't trust the cleanliness of it and I damn sure wasn't trying to lie in a bed that other niggas had been in.

When I met up with females it was at my club or hotels only. Nobody came to my house; I had major trust issues but with Honey I didn't.

The first time I stayed in her apartment I knew I could trust her. Her apartment was clean and well looked after. While she was in the shower I walked around and scoped out the place. Her hamper had a few dirty clothes in it but nothing major. Her kitchen was spotless, the food in the refrigerator smelled and looked good, so I knew momma could cook. Her bed smelled fresh, including the mattress. There were no marks on her carpet; momma was clean. So, when she offered for me to stay, I didn't hesitate. I knew she had just moved and knew I was the only nigga she was dealing with since she moved, so I didn't have to question; I knew I was the only nigga who would have slept in her bed.

We still hadn't made love yet but we continued with our kissing and rubbing sessions. Ma was driving me crazy but in a good way. I used a lot of willpower not to lay pipe to her but when that right moment came, I wasn't holding back.

After a month, I was ready to bring Honey deeper into my world. I asked her to spend the weekend with me to meet my kids. She agreed, but being the woman that she was, she agreed only if I let Monae know that she was going to be around our kids. I respected Honey for that but she gave Monae too much credit. She didn't deserve that courtesy, and if it was up to me, I wouldn't tell Monae shit. But I promised Honey that I would.

"Hey, baby," I greeted her with a kiss and grabbed her duffle bag. She quickly locked up her door and grabbed onto my hand as I walked her down to my car. I couldn't wait to get her home with me so I could share my world with her. I know my kids will be so happy to meet her.

She nervously shook her legs as we rode down to my house; I liked that she was anxious about meeting my kids. It made me see that she cared what they thought about her and it was important to her. Her accepting my kids was a step closer in deepening our relationship.

When I pulled up at my gated mansion, I pressed my fingerprint on the panel opening the gate. Honey smiled at my seven-bedroom mansion with indoor and outdoor pools, a game room for the kids, an indoor basketball court, a theater room, eight bathrooms, and a pool house. I had gold and white decor throughout. I liked white because it represented cleanliness to me and gold was wealth.

I unlocked the door and allowed Honey to go in before me. "Your home is so beautiful Ky-mani," she smiled at me.

"Thank you, Ma. Please feel at home," I said.

She started to look around the house, so I went and dropped her bag into my room.

Monae texted me to say she was on her way over. I had texted her earlier to say I needed to talk to her about something. All I know is she had better not be on any bullshit or I would put her ass out.

I went off to find Honey and found her sitting on the couch waiting for me.

"The kids are on their way," I said and she nodded. "Don't be nervous; they're just kids," I laughed, signaling for her to come to me.

"They're your kids, Ky-mani. If they don't like me then it will spoil everything. I know they're your kids so they must come first and I would not expect you to stay with me if they didn't want you to," she said and I had to laugh.

"That's why I know that they're going to like you because you are so kind and thoughtful, Honey. But they could never stop me from seeing you. I'm their daddy, not the other way around. I won't allow a six-year-old and four-year-old dictating to me," I said and rubbed her on the back.

"So, I was thinking that we could swim with the kids when they arrive," I said and she smiled and kissed me on the lips.

"Ok, I will go and get changed," she said.

I pulled her in for a hug and walked her to my room.


"Whoa, that's a big bed," she laughed at my California-sized four poster bed that was huge. I built steps for it so my kids could get in bed with me.

She grabbed her bag and pulled out her clothes looking for her bathing suit. Every item she pulled out, I put in a spare drawer in my dresser. "Saves you looking for things," I said when she looked up at me.

She picked up her peach two-piece bathing suit and showed it to me. "Hmm, I can't wait to see that on you," I said, taking a seat on the bed.

I watched as she removed her clothes and underwear.

She looked so goddamn good. Her skin was flawless and glistened like chocolate silk. She had a huge peach shaped booty that I couldn't keep my hands off. Her waist was tiny, sculptured in a perfect hour glass shape that then dropped into her hips that were wide and shapely like that shit was drawn. Her thighs were thick and delicious.

And she had the prettiest breasts I had ever seen; firm perky mountains with chocolate drop nipples.

I looked down to see that she was perfectly waxed as always with one stripe of hair. My baby was the baddest chick I had ever seen.

She went to pick up her bottoms but I pulled it out of her hand. It had been many years since the taste of pussy touched my tongue and I was dying to experience that taste again.

"Do you trust me, Honey?" I asked and she nodded her head.

"I promise I won't penetrate you. I just want to taste you," I whispered and pulled her towards me. I kissed her, pushing my tongue into her mouth, and caressed her soft breasts with my hands.

7

I gently pushed her down onto my bed and kissed her again. I kissed and licked down her body until I found her nipples. I flicked and twirled my tongue around them and pulled them into my mouth. She arched her back and dug her fingers into my hair. She moaned and groaned as I sucked harder on her breasts.

I licked my way down her body until I reached my prize. I gently parted her legs as far as they would go, and then plunged my tongue into her. I flicked my tongue back and forth over her clit before pulling it into my mouth and sucking on it.

"Oh, Ky-mani!" she moaned and tugged on my hair.

I dipped my tongue inside of her and drank up her juices. Damn ma tasted sweet like pineapples. She had me hungry for more and more. I pulled her legs and wrapped them around my head pulling me deeper into her goodness. I licked up and down her opening and rubbed my nose into it. She smelled like pineapples too. She just smelled and tasted sweet like honey; so, fresh, so addictive.

She gripped the sheets and groaned out loud. I grabbed her legs and kept her in place. I sucked and licked harder as she screamed out.

"Shit, Ky-mani. Fuck!" she cried out. Her juices

started seeping out and I lapped that shit up; it tasted too good to waste.

"Ky-mani, I'm gonna come. I'm gonna come," she hollered.

"Come on then, ma," I said against her pussy. I slipped a finger into her and she screamed out.

"Oh God!!!" she yelled as her pussy let loose and her body convulsed until it went limp.

"Damn, ma, you taste so fucking good," I said, wiping my mouth with some tissue from the side table.

I laughed as she rolled over and curled into a ball. If she was like that over my tongue skills, I felt sorry for her when I laid this monster on her pretty ass. I walked into the bathroom to brush my teeth and washed my face. When I was about to dry it, my doorbell rang. I quickly dried my face off and went back into my room.

"The kids are here," I said, pulling her up to her feet and kissing her before I ran out to get the door.

When I pulled it open, my kids jumped into my arms almost making me fall to the ground.

"Hey, babies," I laughed and picked them up.

"Look at this, Daddy. Grandma got me a Build a Bear doll. Isn't she pretty?" Chyna said, shoving her doll in my face.

"And I got this car, Daddy," Mani said, showing me his car.

"That's nice of grandma," I smiled, putting them back on the ground.

"Who wants to go swimming?" I asked and they jumped up and down shouting at me.

"Alright, go into your rooms and get your bathing suits. I'm gonna come up and get y'all dressed in a minute," I said and they took off running in the house.

"So, you wanted to talk to me, Law?" Monae said smiling.

"Yeah, follow me for a second," I said, leading her to the kitchen. When she came inside, I looked around to make sure Honey wasn't around and pushed the door closed.

"Yeah, Honey is here for the weekend. I wanted her to meet the kids," I said.

"Who's Honey? That bitch who was wearing white at your party?" she asked and I pushed her.

This is why I brought her ass in the kitchen so Honey wouldn't hear her. She had no damn respect.

"Don't call my woman a bitch," I growled.

"Your woman? Law really?" she said. "My kids are not staying here with a woman that I don't know. We are leaving

10

right now," she went to push past me, but I grabbed her by the throat and pushed her up against the wall.

"Listen to me and listen to me fucking good. Honey is a part of my life and if I want her to meet my kids, she will. She was the one who wanted me to tell you out of respect; clearly, she thinks too highly of you because your ass doesn't deserve any fucking explanation from me. Now my kids are going to meet her and there's nothing you can do about it. And if you disrespect her, you will regret it. Don't you even think about calling her outside of her name," I said and pushed her.

"Fine. But I'm stayingtoo."

"No, the fuck you ain't. I don't want you where I lay my head at. Fuck outta here," I waved her off.

"Either I stay too or we are all leaving. I'm their mother and I have that right too," she said. I was done arguing with her and talking with her.

"Fine, but one smart ass move or comment from you and I'm dragging your ass out of here," I pushed past her and left the room.

I found my kids, dressed them, and sent them back downstairs to Monae. I went in search of Honey and found her sitting on my bed in her bathing suit and a t-shirt on top.

"Why are you sitting in here and wearing a t-shirt?" I

11

smiled at her.

"I was waiting until you said it was okay to come down and meet them. And I didn't want everything hanging out in front of the kids," she said, standing up and showing me.

That's my baby right there. Respectable in front of kids too. I wished their momma was like that.

"Come on, baby, let's go," I pulled her towards me and out of the room.

I could feel her nervousness as we descended the stairs. My kids were running amuck as usual and Monae was ignoring them looking at her phone.

Mani turned and looked up at us first and then Chyna stopped and approached us.

"Hi," she smiled at Honey.

"Hi, I'm Honey. What's your name?" she bent down in front of her.

"I'm Chyna, but my daddy calls me Na Na."

"Nice to meet you, Chyna. And what's your name?" she turned to Mani.

"I'm Ky-mani, like my daddy, but people say I'm Mani," he said and Honey giggled.

"Nice to meet you too, Ky-mani. How old are you?"

"I'm this many," he said, putting up four fingers. Honey laughed and congratulated him on putting up the right number of fingers.

"And I'm six. I'm a big girl," Chyna said, cheesing hard like crazy.

"Indeed, you are. So, would you like to go swimming?" Honey asked them and they nodded their heads and grabbed her hands.

She stood up and walked over to Monae.

"Hi, I'm Honey. Nice to meet you," she smiled at Monae.

Monae looked up at me and I gave her a look that made her know not to fuck with me.

"Hey, I'm Monae, and you too," she said, blankly.

"We are going to go swim now. Are you coming to join us?"

"No, I'm good," Monae said with a slight attitude, but Honey just brushed it off and took the kids outside.

I gave Monae another look and then followed Honey outside with my kids. I sat on a lounge chair and watched as they all jumped in the water splashing me a little. When Honey emerged from under the water, she looked so good with her hair wet and curly.

It felt so good watching them play around together. I definitely made the right choice letting Honey meet the kids.

They couldn't get enough of her as they chased her

around the pool and splashed her. I could tell by her laughter that she was enjoying herself with them. I couldn't help but imagine what she would be like as a mother to our children. Yeah, ma had me thinking like that already.

Monae came and sat outside but didn't contribute to the fun and games. I pulled my vest off and jumped in the water with Honey and the kids. They ganged up on me and splashed me. I placed Honey in front of me, using her as a shield.

We continued to laugh and play with each other until it was supper time.

Honey helped me to dry off the kids and put their towel throwovers on. Monae was still on her phone ignoring us. I don't even know why she chose to stay.

"I like you, Honey," Mani said, smiling up at her and holding onto her hand.

"Ahh, Mani, I like you too. And you too, Chyna," she smiled at them.

"No, I really like you, Honey. When I'm five, I'm going to get a job and a car and then you're going to be my girlfriend," this little nigga said and Honey laughed her head off.

"When you're five, huh?" she asked and he nodded his head.

"So, little man, just like that you're gonna steal daddy's

14

girlfriend?" I asked and he smiled up at me.

"Yep, Daddy, sorry," he said and we all laughed.

Honey put the kids down to watch TV as she helped me get dinner started.

We rushed around the kitchen together and prepared steak, mashed potatoes, and sweet corn. Monae's ass didn't even offer to help. She just sat down at the table and grabbed a plate; no thank you, no nothing. I was trying my hardest not to lose my cool but she wasn't helping. I was so close to snapping on her ass and throwing her out.

She sat at the table eating and straight mean mugging Honey. She was such a jealous, pathetic bitch that it was a joke.

After we ate and I cleared everything away, I went to give the kids a bath. I didn't want Honey left alone with Monae, so I made her go and sit up in my room to wait for me.

I ran a bath in the master bathroom in the hall and grabbed them one by one for a bath. "I like Miss Honey, Daddy. She's kind to me and Mani," Chyna said, playing with a doll in the bathtub as I washed her.

"Yeah, I like her too, baby," I said.

When I was done, I brought them in to say good night to Honey and then to their momma.

"Um, Law?" Monae called me.

15

"Go on up and wait for Daddy. I'll be there soon," I told the kids. I couldn't stand their momma, but I didn't want to show it in front of them.

"Yes, Monae."

"Where am I sleeping?" she asked, smiling.

"Come on," I moaned and she got up to follow me.

I lead her to the furthermost guest room from my room and showed her in.

"Have a good night, Monae," I said and turned to walk away but she stopped me.

"Well, where are you sleeping?" she asked.

"In my room with Honey," I said and pulled my arm away from her.

"What? So, you're going to leave me alone and sleep next to her?"

"Yeah. Why? What did you want; me to leave her alone and sleep with you?"

"No, but why can't we all sleep separately?" she asked and I laughed.

"Yeah, so you can sneak your naked ass in my bed? Yeah, I'm good on that. Good night, Monae," I said and walked away.

I went into my kids' rooms and tucked them in before going into my room. Honey had showered and was laid across the bed in a nightshirt. She was lying on her stomach

16

reading her kindle. I climbed on top of her back and rotated my hips into her booty. I kissed her back and she giggled.

"Be right back," I said and jumped up to take a shower.

When I got out, Honey was still on her stomach reading. I cut off the lights, grabbed her kindle, set it down, and then jumped into bed rolling her over and pulling her on top of me.

"I think I'm a little more interesting than a book," I smiled and stroked her face.

"Oh, you're a whole lot more interesting than a book," she smiled and kissed me.

I slipped my tongue into her mouth and she sucked on it and my lips. I pulled up her night shirt and rubbed on her booty. She felt so good. Instantly my dick was hard as a rock. I wanted to feel her so bad, but now wasn't the right time with my kids down the hall.

I pulled her night shirt up and rubbed my hands over her breasts. She grabbed my dick and I froze. I couldn't take anymore. I flipped her over onto her back and lay between her legs.

"Honey, I want to feel you so bad. Can I rub him against your panties?" I whispered and she agreed.

I pulled my shorts down and grabbed my dick. I positioned him so that it was laying on her clit above her

17

panties, and I thrust back and forth rubbing myself against her. Her pussy felt so warm against my dick. I wanted so much more but for now, this felt good. I let a few moans escape my mouth as I closed my eyes. I put my other hand on her breasts and rubbed her nipples in the palm of my hand.

I was really getting into it when I heard a knock at the door.

"Damn," I breathed as I got up, adjusted my dick and approached the door. I made sure Honey had covered herself and then I pulled the door open. Monae was standing there with her hands on her hips. I stepped outside the door and closed it behind me.

"What, Monae?"

"Take me home. I'm not about to lay up in this house with you fucking that bitch like I ain't down the hall. How can you fuck her with me being here?" she whispered with a damn attitude.

"First of all, this is my motherfucking house and my woman. You've come and invited yourself on her weekend and you want to have a goddamn attitude? What you really mad about is that I don't want to lay up with you. But I promise you this; my dick will never ever go near your sneaky pussy again. You wanna go home fine," I said and stormed off into my room.

"Sorry, baby. She wants to go home. She's got an

attitude and a huge fucking problem," I said and grabbed my phone. After doing what I needed to do. I dropped my phone back on the bed and went back out to Monae.

"You wanna go home. An Uber will be outside in fifteen minutes to take your ass home," I said.

"Law? An Uber? Really?" she said.

"Yeah motherfucking right, nobody told your ass to stay so you can take your own ass home."

"Well, I'm not going," she said, folding her arms and I had enough. I grabbed her by the throat and choked her.

"Listen to me! Get. The. Fuck. Out. Now, Monae, or I will put you out. Don't bring your ass to my house anymore. When I want my kids, I will come for them and drop them back off. You bring your ass here again and I will beat your ass. You hear me?" I squeezed and she nodded her head. I let her go and she walked away toward to the guest room.

I waited for her to get her things and then I led her out to the waiting car. She walked through the opened door without another word and I closed the door behind me and reset the alarm.

When I got back into the room, Honey was sitting up in the bed looking worried.

"I'm causing problems, ain't I?" she said.

"No, Honey, never. It's Monae. She thinks because she has my kids that she's entitled to be with me. I had to let her

19

know what time it was. She's their mother and that's it. I don't want any part of her and she needs to get the damn picture," I said, pulling Honey into my arms.

As much as I wanted to continue with our session, Monae had completely fucked up the mood. She was out of her fucking mind. I was supposed to sleep separately from Honey so that her nasty horny ass could try to sleep with me with Honey down the hall; and she called me trifling. So, don't sleep with MY woman, instead, I should fuck my baby momma and not my woman?

This is the prime reason why out of all the town women I could have had, I fucked around with a handful. There were plenty bad bitches I could have fucked, but the reason that I didn't was because there were females who would go crazy once they got the dick and I didn't want the troubles.

I fucked with the bitches who wouldn't do shit once I no longer had any interest in seeing them. And that's why I didn't fuck with Monae like that because I knew her ass was capable of doing some psycho shit and I knew I shouldn't have in the first place.

But despite Monae being delusional and crazy, I knew I could control her ass to some extent. She could have kicked off, tried to fight or broke shit, but instead, she left like I told her to. Now if only she listened all the time and stopped

20

watching my dick, we might be able to get along for our kids.

There was no way I was going back there with Monae, whether I had a woman or not; but I damn sure wasn't leaving Honey for her. I had big plans for Honey; she didn't even know.

I wanted us to get married and I wanted to break off a few seeds in her too. And the sooner the better. Maybe that would calm Monae's ass down. She felt obligated to be my woman because she had the kids, well what if Honey had my kids too? Would she still feel obligated?

"I'm thinking maybe tomorrow I should take you to meet my mom and sisters," I said to Honey, rubbing her back.

"Really, Ky-mani? You're ready for me to do that?" she asked.

"Of course, Honey. I've been ready."

"Oh okay, that's fine if you want to," she said and snuggled into me.

I was more than ready for her to meet my family because after that, wasn't anything else left to do and nothing to stop me from giving her my seeds. Since I spoke to Killa a few weeks back, he had not made any appearances and he hadn't been following her anymore. I knew who he was from the jump; I saw him in his car leaving my birthday party so I put Ricky on his ass. It was the main reason why I stayed with Honey that night after our date. He was under the fucking impression that I was going to leave Honey that night so he could have gotten to her.

I had to shut that shit down quick. And while he was at bay for the moment, having Honey pregnant would guarantee his ass being gone.

Hmmm – now that's a thought!

# Chapter Two

### *Honey*

Ky-mani's kids were so cute and I can't believe I finally met them. Chyna looked just like Ky-mani; same face, same skin tone, some long hair, everything. I couldn't help but laugh when she screwed up her face the same way her daddy did. It was too funny.

And then Mani with his little cute self. He may not have looked much like Ky-mani but he had his ways and mannerism. He looked just like his momma though, red boned and all. He had a crush on me and I found it hilarious that big Ky-mani and little Ky-mani had a thing for me.

And then there was Monae. I couldn't believe it when I turned around and was face to face with the same lady in red from Ky-mani's birthday party. That woman did nothing but stare my ass down the whole night. She may have been his baby momma, but I had nothing to do with the fact that they weren't together when I met him. She couldn't blame me for him not wanting to be with her.

That bitch straight ignored my ass all day and

complained about me. Ky- mani had been trying his best to protect me but I heard the way she spoke about me. I shouldn't have been surprised because she was exactly how he said she would be; petty, disrespectful, immature, and with the worst attitude ever. I didn't care, though; her words couldn't hurt me.

Oh my God and before I forget, Ky-mani's tongue game was the one! He sucked the soul out of my pussy. Even after I came, my body still quivered with aftershocks like a fucking earthquake had hit me. I had to ball up just to catch myself. I've been thinking about taking the dick for a while now, but I'm not sure that I will be ready for it! It's funny how when a guy wants to wait for someone, all you want to do is give it to him. Sometimes when we kiss and mess around, I want him to just take it but he hasn't.

For me, his patience is what turns me on the most and makes me want to wrap it up in bows and hand it to him.

But despite that I am so happy. Things were going great; even Jerome disappeared after Ky-mani spoke to him and I was happy about that. When I saw his face, I didn't feel a single thing. All I kept thinking about the whole time he spoke to me was, *I hoped Ky-mani didn't see me and think I was actually talking to Jerome and then leave me.*

That says it all when you look into the face of a man

who you've spent five years with, lost your virginity to, planned to marry, and have kids with; and all you could do was think about the new man in your life. The love was gone.

It did surprise me though when he grabbed me and I turned and saw Jerome instead of Killa. But all that was too little and too late. He should have done it when I still had an interest in him, not when I moved on to bigger and better things. I was trying to move forward with my life not backward. Like I said; too little, too late.

We were all up early, washed, and dressed in house clothes. The kids and I sat down to eat breakfast before going to visit Ky-mani's mom as he ran into town. I put his breakfast up and ate with the kids. I made pancakes, sausages, eggs, and a fruit salad.

After we ate, I cleaned up, then sat in the living room and played with the kids until Ky-mani returned.

As much as I loved being around them and helping Ky-mani with them, I felt a little sadness. I wasn't quite ready for kids yet, but I did want some one day. I imagined what it would be like to have some. But the only two men that I found in my life already had theirs; Jerome with his herd of kids and now Ky-mani with his two. He never mentioned wanting anymore and I doubt that he did but if he did, he already had a boy and a girl, so what would be the surprise or need in having any more? Maybe I wasn't supposed to and I could come to terms with that, as long as I could love and spoil Ky-mani's kids as my own, I was good with that.

The kids took off running when they heard the front door open. They jumped all over Ky-mani before he could even finish walking through the door.

"Daddy, Daddy, Honey taught us how to make pancakes, Daddy. And then we made smiley faces on it with our fruit. It was yummy, Daddy," Chyna sang excitedly.

"Yeah and I made you ,Daddy, but then I ate you," Mani said and laughed.

"Boy, you did what? Ah, remind me to get you back," Ky-mani tickled him. He really was a good dad. I loved how he bathed them, read to them, and taught them. He actually spent time with them, not like some men who had their kids but that's as far as it went.

"Hey, babe," he said and gave me a kiss.

"Ohhh, Daddy," the kids said and we started laughing.

"Come on, let me get your breakfast for you," I said, taking the bags from his hand and walking into the kitchen. He took a seat at the breakfast bar and I warmed up his plate.

"Orange juice?" I asked and he nodded. I took down a

tall glass and filled it.

"Thank you, baby," he said when I placed it down in front of him. The microwave stopped and I took out the plate and placed it down in front of him too.

"Hmm smells so good, baby, but you smell better," he said, yanking me down onto his lap. He stuck his nose into my neck and sniffed me.

"Hmmm, Honey, what are you doing to me?" he said, rubbing my hand against his rock-hard erection.

I continued to rub it for him as he ate his breakfast.

"Baby, you are so lucky, I swear," he chuckled and pushed his dick further into my hand. He gave my booty a quick smack and nibbled on my ear causing me to giggle.

"Come on, let me show you what I bought and then get ready to leave because my ma keeps blowing up my phone," he laughed.

I grabbed the bags and followed him to his room. He took the bags from my hand and emptied its contents on the bed. I laughed out when I saw what he had bought.

He bought a white linen man's shorts set for himself, a white linen summer dress for me, and little versions for the kids.

"Oh, we about to be on matching point," I laughed and he nodded.

"Yep, we'll be stepping in style as a family," he said. "Oh yeah, and these are for you, madam," he said, picking up a shoe box and handing it to me. I opened it and he had bought me a pair of white gladiator sandals.

"Thank you, Ky-mani," I leaned and kissed him.

"You're welcome. Now you and Chyna get dressed in here and Mani and I will get dressed in his room," he said and ran out the room.

"Oh is that my dress?" Chyna asked as she walked in.

"Yep and it looks just like mine. Are you ok with that?" I asked and she grinned widely.

"Yes, we are going to be twins today," she said and climbed up on the bed.

I pulled off her clothes and helped her into her dress. I grabbed a brush and gently pulled her hair into a side-swept high ponytail using a big, white bow to tie it. I placed a white headband with flowers at the front. I slipped on her white Prada sandals and she was ready.

She ran over to look in the mirror. "Oh, I like it," she said, swaying the dress back and forth.

"You look pretty, Chyna," I said.

I gathered up my dress and went into the bathroom to change into it. I don't know if he looked at my clothes size before he left but he got the perfect size. It fit nicely on my

28

bodyand stopped a little above my knees.

When I went back into the room, he and Mani were looking so sweet in their matching outfits and sneakers. Ky-mani had bought him a pair of all white Air Forces that matched his.

"Ohhh I got good taste," Ky-mani said when he saw me standing at the door.

"Yeah you do. I love this dress," I smiled.

"I was talking about you, Honey," he said and I laughed.

My hair was already styled from this morning when I washed it and applied mousse to it; so I grabbed my earrings and watch, threw on some eyeliner and mascara, and then I was ready to roll.

Mani grabbed my hand and Chyna took her daddy's and we strolled out the house. Ky-mani loaded us up in his black Range and we headed off to his momma.

I was so nervous. Ky-mani seemed like he loved and valued his momma more than anything; she was his world. And we all know how meeting the mother-in-law can be like sometimes. If she hates me I just know Ky-mani would pick her over me. All I could do was pray that this wouldn't be the last time that I saw Ky-mani because I was feeling him something strong.

His momma lived outside of town in River North, not

too far from where I was brought up with my momma. She lived in a beautiful gated complex that had the initials DP and MP on the huge black gates. Ky-mani used his fob to open up the gates. He drove up the spiraled pathway and stopped at the top beside the house.

"What's DP and MP stand for?" I asked.

"My parents' initials, Doreen and Malik Parker," he said proudly.

The house was beautiful. It was a beautiful pink mansion surrounded by rose bushes and immaculately groomed grass.

He took the kids out of their seats and grabbed my hand leading me to the house. He used his keys to open the huge, brown double doors.

"Momma, we're here," he yelled into the hall. I was in awe of the beauty of the house. It had high ceilings that were dressed with crystal chandeliers, and it was decorated in brown wood flooring and cream walls and furniture. There was a huge fireplace with a sixty-inch TV mounted above it.

I turned when I heard footsteps coming towards us.

I saw the same lady I saw him with on TV. She was a beautiful woman with long, curly hair, that she had pinned up and the same chocolatey complexion as Ky-mani.

"Hey, Grandma's babies," she sang and the kids ran over to her. She kissed them and continued walking towards us.

"Hey, son, about time you got here. I thought you were going to have me waiting here all day," she kissed him on the cheek.

"And you must be Honey, sweetie?" she said before wrapping her arms tightly around me. "Welcome to the family," she said, kissing me on my cheek.

"Nice to meet you, Mrs. Parker," I said and she shook her finger at me.

"Uh huh. None of that Mrs. Parker malarkey, you can call me Momma Doreen and only because I'm not trying to replace your mother at all. Ok?" she smiled at me and hugged me again.

"Come on in the house and make yourself at home," she told me, leading me further into her beautiful home.

When I walked into the living room, I was faced with four more family members. I thought I only had to meet his two sisters? I swallowed hard and continued walking in.

They all immediately got up and approached me.

"Wow, bro, she's beautiful. Go Ky-mani," a short, young looking girl with long, straight hair said eyeing me.

"This is my baby sister, Toya," Ky-mani said, introducing us.

"Hey, Honey, my brother is feeling you hard; he talks about you all the time. You got him sprung," she whispered loud to me and winked as she pointed at Ky-mani. He pushed her away and told me to ignore her.

"Hi, Honey, I'm Nevaeh," a medium height beautiful girl said, hugging me. "Don't mind, Toya, she talks before she thinks," she laughed.

Next, I was introduced to Momma Doreen's sister, Ruth. She and Momma Doreen almost looked like twins but she was a little older, which I could only tell from her eyes. They glowed with a little, gray ring that she got as she grew older.

"This is Aunt Ruth, Ricky's momma," Ky-mani said and we shook hands.

Lastly, I was introduced to a tall, muscular man, with long braids and hazel eyes. He looked at me and compared to everyone else, he didn't seem too happy to meet me.

"This is my Unc, Marco Ramsey, Aunt Ruth's husband," Ky-mani said.

Marco shook my hand quickly and went back to his seat.

"Let's go outside," Momma Doreen suggested, so we followed her out onto the patio. There was a brown hooded gazebo with tied back white drapes with ten chairs surrounding a brown, round table. It overlooked a huge, rectangular swimming pool and more rose bushes.

I grabbed a seat next to Ky-mani and his sister, Toya, took the other one next to me.

"So, Honey, how old are you?" she asked, resting her chin on her hand and leaning over closely to me.

"Twenty-three," I replied.

"Twenty-three? You do realize this grandpa is Twenty-nine, right?" she teased and laughed.

"Yo, who are you calling grandpa?" Ky-mani yelled out. "Watch it Toya or I will beat that ass," he threatened her and she sucked her teeth and rolled her eyes.

"So y'all gonna get married and have some babies?" she asked.

"Yo, Toya, for real Ma chill and stop trying to scare Honey off," he said and waved his hand at me to ignore her.

"What? I'm trying to help you out, bro. She's way better than those chicken heads I've seen you talk to and that damn Monae," she screwed up her face and said. "About time you gave me a pretty ass sister-in-law that I can actually talk to and walk on the streets with," she laughed but Ky-mani didn't.

33

"Momma!" he yelled out.

"Toya, leave that girl alone and mind your business. She probably won't want to marry him now so she can get away from your little nosey ass," Momma Doreen said and we all started laughing.

"Momma's boy," Toya whispered to Ky-mani and stuck her tongue out at him.

"Sorry about that, now you know why I took so long for you to meet them," he laughed and squeezed my thigh under the table.

We sat and ate with his family, talking about life and sharing jokes. It felt so nice being around them and being welcomed by them, especially as my family was in another state.

I came from a small family; just me, my momma, and my grandparents. I had a few cousins from my grandma's sister's children, but we were a small family. But since my grandpa died a year ago, it left only my momma and grandma in Texas. My grand-aunt, Julia, lived in Miami with my momma's cousin, Christine, and her five kids. I used to visit with them often when I was growing up. Because we were a small family and I had no siblings, I always wanted a big family. Ky-mani didn't have a huge family but it was nice to be amongst different members of it.

Throughout the day, Ky-mani's demeanor changed from that of a happy one to a pissed off one. After telling me he was fine the whole day, he finally told me that Monae was acting up and demanding he bring the kids back even though he had another day with them.

So, he decided to end our visit and drop the kids off home.

His family gave me warm hugs and kisses and told me to visit again. Well, all of them except Marco that is.

When we got into Ky-mani's car and drove away, I decided to ask him what was up with his uncle.

"Oh don't worry about Marco. Unc doesn't trust any female around me, especially after Monae's ass. He's just looking out for me. He does that all the time; even when I started hanging with KY and Drake, he didn't trust them. It took him a minute to get used to them," he said and I finally understood. He was just protecting his family and even I could understand that.

Ky-mani looked so angry as he drove towards Monae's house. I felt like she was punishing him because of me.

"Ky-mani, you should take me home so you can spend your time with the kids. We can see each other another day," I said and he lifted my hand and kissed the back of it.

"No, Honey, that's what she wants and I'm not feeding

35

into it. She has no right to demand anything. The kids were going to go home in the morning anyway so that you and I could spend some time together. So, she's only changed the plans by a few hours. She doesn't want the kids' home; she wants me to take you home. But I'm going to give her exactly what she doesn't want," he smiled at me and stroked my face.

Before long we were at Monae's house. She lived in the heart of town on a little cul-de-sac. The kids had fallen asleep. I offered to help him but Ky-mani thought it would be best if I just waited in the car. He pulled Chyna from her car seat and carried her to the door. After knocking and waiting for a few seconds, Monae opened the door.

Without saying a word to her, he passed her and went into the house with Chyna. She stood by and watched him before turning her attention to me in the car.

Seconds later, Ky-mani emerged from the house and grabbed Mani from his seat and passed Monae again. When he was done, he walked back to the car, climbed in, and drove away without saying a single word to her.

I didn't know what to say, so I said nothing.

When we got back to his house, he had finally calmed down. "Sorry about earlier but I just don't like Monae, I never did. And I hate how she uses my kids against me as a tool. I don't even know how she got pregnant, Honey. I never slept with her without a condom. And I only slept with her a handful of times; it just doesn't make any sense. But that's my fault for even sleeping with her in the first place," he said, wrapping his arms around my waist.

"Let's go to bed, ma. I just want to lay up under you," he said, pulling me to his room. After taking a shower together, he pulled me into him tightly and buried his head into my back.

Despite Monae playing games, we had a good weekend. We spent all day Sunday laid up in bed just talking until he dropped me back home.

As I laid in bed, I couldn't help but feel like despite how good and happy Ky-mani and I were, how good it felt to meet his family, and they welcomed me, I couldn't shake a feeling like things were about to change!

# Chapter Three

*Monae*

I am so tired of this bitch! When Ky-mani texted me to say he needed to talk to me I was happy. I imagined us talking and then talking leading to fucking. I was so excited that I wasted no time getting ready. I put on a sexy, short summer dress that showed off my legs and breasts. Plus, it was free flowing, so that would make it easier for Ky-mani to pull up.

On my way over in a taxi, I imagined him giving me the dick down in his room. I imagined it to the point I almost orgasmed right there in the fucking taxi.

So, imagine my despair when he told me he just wanted to tell me that Honey was spending the weekend with him so she could meet my fucking kids. The lump that formed in my throat when he called her his woman threatened to choke the life out of me. I was beyond distraught. They went from meeting, to her being his woman in a month! And here I was nine fucking years later and still just the kids' momma.

When that pretty bitch came, and greeted me, I wanted to smack the taste out of her mouth. She was so much prettier in person and up close, with flawless skin that didn't need any makeup. Her eyes sparkled and enhanced her beauty so much more. It hurt to see that he picked a prettier and younger bitch over me. Ky-mani and I were the same age so I felt a major kind of way staring at this twenty-something-year-old goddess.

She had on a bathing suit that made her body look like God himself sculptured it, even with a t-shirt covering it. I could just imagine the joy he must be having being knee deep in her pussy. That thought had knots forming in my stomach.

The way she played with the kids came so naturally to her; I wished I was like that. I loved my kids because they were a part of Ky-mani but I couldn't relate to them. Everything I did with them was regarding Ky-mani and if he wasn't able to see them, then I brought them to my grandma. I didn't have a relationship with my momma, but I did with my grandma mainly because they didn't speak to each other either. My grandma didn't blame me for Pete, she blamed him saying I was young and he took advantage but we all know that it was me.

I loved my kids but I resented them at the same time which is probably why I didn't spend time with them, or did anything with them. I resented them because they got all of Ky-mani's love and attention and I got nothing. And now I had to compete with this new bitch!

She was so damn perfect with her pretty ass, walking around cooking and cleaning and shit. And he looked like a fucking king doting on his queen. He wanted me to go home and leave my kids here with his bitch so they could play happy family. Fuck no!

I put my foot down and he accepted it. But there was a method to my madness. Well, there would have been if he didn't come and shit on it by putting me in the last guestroom and going back to his room with her!

Since I had my kids I've tried everything in the book to get to stay over and he never ever allowed it not even once. His excuse was his time with the kids was for him alone. Yet here he was sharing it with her and allowing her to sleep in his house after only a few weeks of knowing her. Not only did she embarrass me by showing up matching him and standing in my place beside him at his birthday party, but now she had worked her way into my spot once again.

I admit, I cried like a damn baby when he put my ass in the guest room and went with her. I had planned to sneak into the room he was sleeping in and try to fuck him and if he did, I planned on being real loud so she could hear me and if he didn't I was going to argue loudly with him so she would see me leaving his room naked and make it look like he lured me into his room to fuck. But there was no way I could do that with them sharing a room.

I left the room to walk around hoping he was still awake somewhere in the house, but as I went to walk past his room, I heard him moaning. He was enjoying her and fucking her like I wasn't even there! I couldn't hear her moaning, only him. At least she had some kind of respect for me being there and I could imagine that she was suppressing her sounds but he didn't give a fuck. It was like he wanted me to hear him.

I don't know what got into me, but before I knew it I was banging on the door.

When he swung it open I envied the bitch something hard. He looked so fucking fine shirtless standing there in his basketball shorts. I could see that his dick was still hard from fucking her. And my heart broke. Yes, I've obviously fucked him before but he was always clothed. Never naked, shirtless, nothing. I had never seen his body until that point. She had him in a way that others wished they did. She had his heart, his body, his soul, and his dick; whereas all we got was his dick without any meaning or feelings.

I was so hurt when he called an Uber and put me out. I went home with pure rage in my heart for the bitch. She needed to go; I hated her with a passion. I hated her so much that if I knew where her momma lived, I would have killed the bitch for making such a pretty motherfucker.

In the morning, I sat alone in my house, no kids and no Ky-mani. They were out enjoying themselves and giving their time to Honey. Even his family wanted to entertain the bitch. I was never taken to his momma's house or any of his family for that matter. I only met them when he brought them to my home to explain that I was pregnant but they never ever liked me. My rep from before ruined any chance I had with him; his family knew who I was and they hated me for him.

I wished that I had met Law first before I did all that pregnancy scam shit with those other men. I wondered if maybe he would have been with me or at least fucked me properly.

I hated my kids being out with them, so I texted Ky-mani and told him to bring my damn kids home. I didn't really want them home; what I wanted was for him to take that bitch home instead. I wanted him to diss her for me even if it was just once, but no he didn't. He put me in my place by showing up at my house and dropping the kids off.

When I opened the door, he pushed right past me without saying a single word to me. I noticed he had on a white linen suit and Chyna had on a white linen dress. When he carried Mani in after, I noticed he had on a little linen suit that looked like Ky-mani's.

Curiosity got the best of me and when he opened the car door to climb back in, I got a smack in the face when I noticed she too had on a white linen dress like Chyna.

This motherfucker had them all dressed similarly as a family! How could he do that?

I ran to the bathroom and threw up until my stomach hurt. She was replacing me and taking my life. Sure, I could just take the back seat and stay in the baby momma lane obediently like he wanted me, to but I wouldn't be me if I did that. I didn't do settling, I did all or nothing. I wanted Law in every way possible and all to myself!

I say it again...that bitch has to go!!!

\*\*\*

Today was Monday and I was still reeling from the weekend. Ky-mani had me all the way fucked up. He messed up my weekend so I was about to fuck his day up just because I could. When I dropped the kids off I told the school that their father was supposed to be collecting them and I went about my day.

I called my girls, ordered some food and drinks, and waited for Ky-mani to catch up to me. We were drinking, eating, and having a good old time when my phone rang. I cut the music off and signaled for my girls to keep quiet as I answered.

"Hi, Law," I sang sweetly.

"Don't hi Law me, why is the fucking school calling me telling me I'm late to collect the kids. Where the fuck your ass at?" he roared.

"I'm helping my grandma, Law. I thought you said you were collecting the kids today," I said and held my laughter in.

"Monae, you know damn well I never told your ass no bullshit like that! I've got deliveries coming at my club and my fucking restaurant. How the hell am I supposed to get the kids and deal with this shit here?" he said and I was killing myself laughing.

"I'm sorry, Law. I thought you said so. But my car isn't working remember, so by the time I leave and travel there it will be even later."

"Bye, Monae. Just make sure your ass is there when I drop them off later," he said and hung up.

My girls and I started laughing.

"Good. Let that nigga run around you now," Tessa said and dapped me up.

"You know he's gonna beat your ass, right?" Trina laughed and I rolled my eyes.

"Oh please, the nigga just needs some pussy and all will be forgiven," I said.

When he dropped the kids off later I was going to throw the pussy at him; if I had to hold on to his leg to get him to fuck me I was. In fact, I was going to let him in to drop the kids off and lock the door. And the only way he could get out was to fuck me.

Call it what you like, but I was desperate, and I needed to go to desperate measures.

We continued to talk about shit and they were getting ready to leave so I could get ready for Law. But then he started to ring me again.

"Hi, Law."

"What time are you going to be back? Honey has the kids at the mall and she's going to drop them home for me," he said but I saw red and flipped my lid!

"She what?! Why the fuck does your bitch have my motherfucking kids, Law? Bring me my kids and you better not let her do it."

"Who the fuck do you think you're talking to like that, bitch? I got a good mind to fuck your ass up! I needed help. Honey was there for me unlike your thot ass running the streets instead of being a fucking mother to your kids!" he yelled but I hung up on his ass.

"What's wrong?" Trina said.

"That bitch is at the mall with my kids. He made her ass pick them up talking about she dropping them off. Like hell she is. Let's go, I'm gonna beat her motherfucking ass, I've had enough," I spat as I grabbed my keys.

Law kept calling me but I was ignoring his ass. If he wasn't bringing my kids home, that bitch sure wasn't. Once again she was getting in the way of my feelings and my plans. But not anymore.

I wanted to see what homegirl was going to do with three against one.

The whole ride over my blood was boiling. We all removed our earrings and pulled our hair up. That bitch wasn't escaping without getting a beat down; then her ass would think twice about going to collect my fucking kids. Law kept calling my ass but I didn't care; I wanted blood and it was hers I was after.

We rushed through the mall looking high and low for this bitch and then I spotted her. She had the audacity to be holding my kids' hands like she was their fucking mother. I raced over to her and stood in her face. Automatically my girls went on either side of her; this bitch wasn't escaping me today.

"Bitch, why the fuck you got my kids?" I barked at her and she stopped walking and looked up at me.

46

"Excuse me, Monae," she said.

"You heard what the fuck I said."

"Ky-mani asked me to collect them for him because you weren't around and he was stuck working," she said and folded her arms.

"I don't give a fuck. I'm their momma, not you."

"You could have fooled me," she scoffed.

This bitch was pretty confident for someone who was about to get a fucking beat down. I banged my fist in my hand and she laughed. Let's see if he still thought her ass was pretty after I fucked up her face.

"Kids let's go now," I called to them but they held on to Honey's hands tighter.

"No Mommy. Daddy said we could go with Honey; she going to take us for some ice cream," Chyna said.

That only made me want to beat the bitch's ass more. She had my fucking kids wanting to stay with her too.

"Kids, you see that play area right there?" she said to my kids, pointing at a little kids' area just to the left of us.

"Yes," they said together.

"Do me a favor and go play there for a second; let me talk to your momma for a minute," she instructed and Chyna took Mani's hand and they ran off together.

"So you really want to fight me, Monae?" she chuckled like I was a joke.

47

"Oh it won't be no fight, Honey; it will be us three kicking your ass," I shot back.

"Monae, walk away. Don't make my job fool you. Now go on because you damn sure don't want none of this," she said as a matter of fact.

"Sis, you good?" I heard and I looked up to see Toya and Nevaeh standing next to Honey.

"Yeah I'm good," she said and smiled at them.

"Monae, what the fuck you want? You think you're about to fight Honey or something, bitch?" Toya said and advanced towards me but Honey pulled her back.

"I'm good, Toya, but do me a favor please, go and check on the kids; they're just over there," she said and pointed at where they were.

This bitch had some balls. She acted like we weren't going to fight her and instead of taking the back-up, she sends one away.

"Monae, I don't have time for your shit, so back the fuck up," she said. Nevaeh stood straight mugging my ass; I knew she wanted to fight me for the longest, so this was the perfect excuse to. I didn't want to fight Law's bitch and sister on the same day but I couldn't walk away now and look like a fool.

"Monae, we both know this isn't about your kids,

48

otherwise they wouldn't have been left at the school for you to do other things."

"Bitch, you don't know what you're talking about. This is about the principle of things, you're not their momma and I damn sure didn't give your ass permission to touch them, even if Law did," I lied because she was right, this was about Law and the fact she had him and I didn't.

"Monae, I'm not going to be any more kinds of bitches. Don't call me outside of my name; I'm addressing you by yours," she said and I laughed.

"Or what...bitch?" I said.

Next thing I knew, this bitch gave me a punch to my throat cutting off my air. She moved so quick I didn't even see her move. I started choking and coughing trying hard to breathe. Tears came to my eyes as I fought to breathe.

"Don't you ever call me a bitch again," she bent down and whispered in my face.

"Say bye to mommy, kids," she sang as she walked away with my kids.

It took me a moment to get back up to my feet. So much for my friends; they just stood there and watched the bitch wind me with one punch. People were crowding around, laughing and filming me. I was so embarrassed. Law's sisters just laughed and walked away with Honey and my kids.

I stood to my feet and walked out of the mall. When we walked back to the car, she was waiting around, probably for Law, but I didn't need his ass coming down and making me even more embarrassed in front of all these people, so I left to deal with him later.

Tessa dropped me back home but she didn't even say a damn word. Trina kept staring at me and asking if I was ok but I didn't answer her.

I hoped Law knew he had some undercover assassin bitch in his life. That wasn't a lucky punch, that bitch knew what she was doing and aimed dead for my throat.

When I got in my house, I headed straight to a mirror. My eyes were bloodshot and I could see a black bruise forming under them. This bitch fucked me up with one punch? That shit made me mad as fuck.

Between Law choking me a few days ago and Honey hitting me, I felt like I had been through a war and back.

How could Tessa and Trina do nothing but stand there? All the bullshit they spat about fucking her ass up, when we were on our way there, to do absolutely nothing at all when it came down to it.

I sat down on my couch and closed my eyes. My head

was banging.

Seconds later and my door was being kicked and banged on so I knew it was Law.

I managed to just unlock it before he pushed it open.

"Monae, you and your bitches tried to jump Honey!!!" he roared so loud it hurt my ears.

"That bitch had no right to have my kids," I countered and he raised his hand like he wanted to hit me and I flinched.

"Call my woman a bitch one more time, Monae. I don't give a fuck how you feel; you will respect her!" he pointed in my face.

"So your ass was busy, but yet you managed to make it to the mall in five minutes to fight Honey, but you couldn't get to the school that's by the mall?" he said and I couldn't even respond.

"That's what I thought. Your ass is trifling," he said and shook his head at me.

He opened the door and got my kids from the car. He kissed them good night and went to walk out of the house but I stopped him.

"So you not gonna say anything about your woman hitting me? Look at my face and eyes. I should press charges," I shouted and he stopped and turned to face me.

"Good, she should have fucked your ass up and knocked

51

some sense into you. You talk about your kids this and that but was you thinking about your kids when you flew down there ready to fight in front of them and cussing all kinds of words? That's the shit you want my kids to see?" he said and I went quiet.

"There you are defending the fact that she hit me."

"Monae, your ass should have never gone down there in the first place. You went down there with two friends. So, you wanted Honey to take your ass whooping but you want to cry about her giving you one punch? Get the fuck out of here with that."

"I don't want her around my kids, Law. She's dangerous, she aimed for my throat; she knew what she was doing. How do you know she won't hit the kids?" I said and he slammed his car door and approached me.

"First of all, Honey loves my kids and she would never do anything to hurt them. She looks out for them more than your ass does. And you want to worry about Honey punching you, if it was me, I would have shot your ass, Monae. And only my kids right now are stopping me from doing it. You disrespected me by stepping to my girl but I promise you, even roll your eyes wrong at her and you will have more than Honey punching you to worry about. You feel me, Monae?" he said, flashing his gun on his waist.

I stood and watched as he drove away from me. The fact he even threatened me and showed me his gun had my head fucked up. Not only has he never done that before, but I saw his eyes and he meant it.

But I couldn't deny that he turned me on by doing that. Imagine when I finally get him to be mine, how hard he will go for me.

I smiled because I would just have to find a way to fuck up Honey's life without touching her. Give me an hour and I'm dirty, give me a day...

## Chapter Four

*Law*

When I heard that Monae was down at the mall with her friends looking to fight Honey, I panicked. Not because I thought my girl was soft, but because I know how devious Monae was; and knowing her ass, she would do something dirty to Honey like throw bleach or acid in her face.

I tried to call Monae to threaten her but she straight ignored my ass. I grabbed my gun and jumped in my car and raced to the mall. I was hell bent on shooting Monae's ass for fucking with my life, but when my sisters called to say Honey knocked that bitch on her ass with one punch, that shit had me harder than a motherfucker. I didn't know my baby got down like that but that's exactly what I needed. Honey was the complete package. She was a lady in every aspect of the word but she knew when to go hard and defend herself; which a queen, my queen, would need to do.

When I saw her at the mall, she was all smiles and cool as hell. I kissed the shit out of her. Toya and Nevaeh were impressed with Honey. My sisters were good girls, but they had a little thug in them from me, so I know they were feeling Honey even more. They were willing to jump in the fight after meeting Honey only once, but ma had it like that. You couldn't help but like her once you met her. I was happy that they were bonding. I needed the women in my life to make a strong bond so that if anything ever happened to me, they could defend this family.

When I took my kids home I didn't even hold back my laughter from Monae with her pathetic ass. She tried to play me today and ended up playing herself.

I knew she had something up her sleeve today. I was glad Honey offered to get the kids for me because I did not want to be bothered with Monae. But I had to let her know, her being at Honey's head was not about to play in my books. To me, Honey is me because she's my queen, the woman that I am going to marry and who will have the rest of my kids; so Monae going after her is to go after me.

When I got home, I found Honey sitting in bed reading like nothing happened. "Ma, what happened today?" I asked and she set her kindle down.

"I'm sorry. I just snapped, Ky-mani. She was being so disrespectful calling me all kinds of bitches. I've done nothing but be respectful to this woman, but I'm not a female

55

who takes disrespect very well, Ky-mani. And she had the audacity to bring friends to try and jump me, which she would have done in front of the kids. That pissed me off even more. They are little kids; they don't need to see no violent shit like that," she explained in a raised tone. I knew she was angry talking about it.

"I told her to walk away but she kept on. So, I punched her in the jugular. I didn't think she would have gone down like that. And her stupid ass friends just stood there. So, I grabbed the kids and walked away," she said and I pulled her close and kissed her on the head.

"Where'd you learn to do that anyway?"

"Oh baby, I may be an accountant and not from the streets, but I can throw hands. Especially as I was enrolled in karate as a kid and my mom's cousin has four sons. I used to visit them every summer and they taught me and their sister how to fight. I don't come from a family of weak bitches; we would get our asses beat if a bitch whooped our ass, best believe. And I was more scared of my momma's whooping so I haven't let a bitch or nigga beat me yet," she laughed.

"That's my baby," I laughed. Knowing she could defend herself made me feel good, but I still wasn't taking any chances with her. I would go insane if anything happened to her.

\*\*\*

"Yo, Cuz, what the fuck happened yesterday. Somebody showed me a video of Honey sucker punching Monae's ass," Ricky said, sitting down in my office.

"Oh for real? I didn't know there was a video of it," I laughed, shaking my head.

"Cuz, that motherfucker is all over World Star Hip Hop, for real," he said.

I immediately jumped on my computer to look it up and sure enough, it was there with over 10,000 views. I pressed play and I could hardly contain myself. My baby looked so good fucking Monae's ass up with a mean right hand. She hit that bitch so quick I had to rewind it over and over again.

My cousin and I laughed our asses off. That serves Monae's ass right. She picked a fight with the wrong one; Honey was a thug and didn't even know it. My dick was so hard from seeing that.

"I don't know what she did to get Honey that angry, but remind me not to fuck with her," Ricky laughed and I joined in.

"Ma, got a little thug in her and I didn't even know. When one of my little niggas called to say some bitches looked like they were about to jump on Honey, nigga, I lost my cool. I grabbed my gun and rushed down there. The fear I felt, nigga, was unreal. If anything happened to Honey I don't know what I'd do, Ricky," I said, shaking my head.

"You love her don't you, Cuz."

"I sure do. She's everything that I need and want, Cuz. She completes me in ways I didn't even know I needed. She's life and I love her so fucking much."

"I feel you, Cuz, and I'm happy for you, trust," he said and I dapped him.

We sat and talked about the girls for a while before he left to make some moves. He was feeling Sydney's ass something deep even though they were just fooling around. I was kind of jealous that he had gotten the pussy the next day after meeting, but I had something so much deeper with Honey and she was well worth the wait.

After all, all good things come to those that wait.

I sat and thought about Honey. She had stayed with me again last night and I dropped her off at work. It felt so good sleeping next to her and waking up seeing her beautiful face. Every time I thought about her going home, it made me sad because I just didn't want to lie down without her. So, I would ask her to stay but for how long would she do that before she wanted to go home?

It was getting to the point that I wanted her to live with me. I know it was soon but I loved her; that I was sure of. My pops always told me when you met 'the one' you would know. He knew it from the first time he saw my momma at the age of sixteen. Just like I knew the second I saw Honey. There was no one I wanted to be with more than her and nowhere I wanted to be but with her. Now that I'd retired from the streets, I had the time to love and I had a lot to give.

Maybe I should just ask Honey to move in with me. I know she was independent and liked her apartment, but what was the point of having it and paying for it, but not using it?

My phone beeped and it was Monae. She caught wind of the video circulating around of Honey hitting her. I don't know what she thought I could or would do about it. No one told her to bring her ass down there trying to fight nobody so her ass deserved it. Maybe she would take her embarrassed ass and sit down somewhere.

I didn't even respond to her.

There was a knock at my door. I put away my books and locked up my safe. I looked down at the monitor and it was my Unc and someone else at my door. I couldn't see his face but I trusted my uncle so I buzzed them in.

"Oh shit, what it do, Cam?" I said and laughed when I noticed that the other person was my uncle's son, Cameron Ramsey. He was the copy of my Unc except for the hazel eyes.

"What up, Law," he said and hugged me.

It had been a few years since I saw Cam. He was originally from Atlanta; he got himself in some trouble and went to jail for three years. I guess his ass was out now.

"Shit, I just touched down; hooked up with my pops and all. But you know I had to see you, young blood. Look at you, all retired and shit, businessman," he said, punching my arm and laughing.

"My bad, what's up, Unc?" I said, dapping my uncle up.

"Oh, you see me now, motherfucker?" he said with an attitude and pushed me aside.

"Sorry, Unc, but it's been a while since I've seen my boy," I said and he flapped his hand at me and sat down firing up a blunt.

"So what's good, Cuz?" Cameron said, jumping in another seat.

"Oh, your cousin in love, Cam. Can you believe that shit?" my uncle said and blew out some smoke.

"Oh for real?" Cam smiled up at me.

"Yeah, Honey is her name. And your pops is straight up hating," I said loudly.

"I'm not hating; I just don't trust people who come into the family. She seems like a nice girl, but nephew you have a habit of attracting crazy ass hoes," my uncle said and Cameron started laughing.

"Come on now, Unc, Honey isn't like that. She hasn't even given me the pussy yet," I said and they both looked at me like I was crazy.

They were fam so I didn't feel ashamed telling them that because I wanted them to see that Honey was different.

"Nigga, you mean to tell me your ass is pussywhipped and you haven't even had the pussy yet?" he laughed, choking on the weed.

"Yep, cause ma has it like that. Ain't no thot gonna hold out on giving pussy," I said.

"True that. Your aunt Ruth made me wait for the longest to get up in her guts," he said and I covered my ears.

"Yo, Unc, enough. I don't need to hear that shit about you with my aunt," I said, screwing up my face.

"But it's okay to hear about you fucking or not fucking your girl? Fuck outta here nephew," he said.

"Yeah but yo ass isn't related to my woman, but I'm related to yours," I said and he sucked his teeth.

"I'm out. You two little motherfuckers, make me sick. Fuck y'all. Enjoy your day with your girl cousin, Cameron. He needs to grow some balls, too scared to get up in his pussy. Later, motherfuckers," he said and walked out of the room.

Cam and I just looked at each other and shook our heads.

"So how does it feel being a free man?" I asked, smiling at him.

"Would have felt better if I could get some pussy in my life; I thought you could help in that field but I guess your ass is on a pussy sabbatical," he said and laughed.

"Nah it's not even like that. I love Honey and I'm trying to do thingsdifferent with her. She's not ready yet and I have to respect that," I said and he nodded.

"For real I respect that."

"Have you seen Ricky? He just left here. I'm sure his hoe ass knows some females," I laughed.

"Oh yeah; how's my little bro doing anyway?"

"He's all good, being a hoe as usual," I laughed.

"Speaking of hoe, how's Monae's stank ass doing?" he said and I laughed.

"Just as fucking annoying as usual. All the bitch does is watch my dick."

"You still fucking her, Cuz?"

"Hell no. I ain't fucked that hoe since she got pregnant with Mani and won't ever again; because all that bitch does is get pregnant even though I'm using a fucking condom," I shook my head.

"Maybe she's poking holes in them, my nigga," he laughed.

"Come on now, Cam, you know me better than that. I never use a condom unless I bought it. These hoes ain't loyal out here and will set a nigga up quick. Look at my ass now, two kids with that bitch."

"You gonna have some kids with Honey? Oh, wait, you do know you actually need to have sex for it to happen, though?" he said, laughing his ass off.

"Nigga, fuck you," I flipped my middle finger up at him and laughed. "But, you straight Cuz; where are you staying at?"

"Nowhere and everywhere, my nigga," he said.

I got up and walked over to my filing cabinets, pulled a key out from the drawer, and handed it to him.

"This is the key to my old house. I never got around to selling it. It's a good house and still has its furniture and all. Consider it a welcome home present," I wrote down the address and handed to him.

"Nah, Cuz, I'm good, I'll make it," he laughed, trying to hand it back but I wouldn't take it.

"Cam, we go way back. We always had each other's backs, so this is me having yours. Plus, you can use it until you get your own," I said, smiling at him.

"Here," I said, handing him a bank card.

"Yo, Law, we fam and all but I ain't your bitch for you to be giving me a fucking bank card. Ain't no pussy between my legs, nigga," he said and I laughed so hard at him.

"That isn't my bank card, nigga," I said and then he looked at it.

During the time that he was in lock up, I opened an account for him and put a pretty amount of money in it. I was the kind of nigga that, if I had money, my family had money, straight. And although he and I shared no blood, my aunt called him her son and for that, he was my cousin and my family.

"Yo, Law, I don't know what to say."

"You don't need to. I know if the tables turned, you would do the same," I hugged him.

"Of course without a doubt."

"Oh shit, are you niggas gonna kiss, hold hands, and sing kumbaya or something? What's up with all this mushy shit?" Drake said as him and KY walked in.

"Man, fuck you. I'm all about pussy, my nigga. Well, I know I am; I don't know about Law's ass acting like a fucking virgin," Cam said.

"Like a virgin touched for the very first time," Drake sang and they all started laughing at me.

"I swear to God I'm about to shoot y'all motherfuckers in a second," I yelled at them still laughing their asses off.

It was all good though because I was definitely going to break this dick off in Honey's ass very soon.

It felt so good having Cam back with us; it was like he never left. He was a good guy; back when I started working for Papa De, Cam was pussy hungry and wasn't interested in what his father did. But I was money hungry, because I knew with money, pussy would follow. He spent most of his time chasing females until he met Desiree. They started fucking around something hard; he loved her but she played him. He found out she was fucking his best friend, Adam.

So, Cameron tried to kill their asses. He shot Adam but they got away before he could kill them. They both pressed charges. He was sentenced to five years but that was reduced as his lawyer argued diminished responsibility.

He was a good guy but pussy was his weakness. As you could see, nigga just touched down and pussy was on his menu before a place to sleep; but I loved him, he was family.

We sat and caught up like old times. I even called Ricky to bring his ass back to see his brother. Cameron was only two years older than Ricky, but older was older in his book; so he called Ricky baby bro that he hated so much.

I chilled with my niggas until it was time to pick up Honey from work.

When she came out, the sight of her warmed my heart. I had missed my baby the whole day. I truly had it bad for her. When she climbed into my car, I pulled her in close and kissed her, running my tongue along her bottom lip. She tasted so good. I ran my hands over her body and grabbed her fat pussy. If we weren't in the parking lot I would have eaten that shit up like my last meal.

"Hey, baby. How was your day?" she asked once I released her lips.

"It was good, baby. My cousin is out of jail and came to see me."

"Oh, that's nice, babe," she kissed my cheek. That's what I loved about her, if something made me happy, she was excited about it.

"How was your day?" I asked and she explained about her day as I drove towards her apartment.

"Oh yeah, you're a celebrity," I told her when she finished talking.

"Why, because I'm your girlfriend?" she giggled.

"Oh no, this one is all you. There's a video circling of you sucker punching Monae," I said and she gasped.

"What? No, you're joking right?"

"Afraid not. It's on YouTube, Facebook, Instagram, and World Star. Look," I said, handing her my phone so she could see the video.

"Oh my God, Ky-mani. I'm so embarrassed. I'm so sorry I did that," she said, shaking her head.

"Honey, you didn't do anything wrong, baby. You had to defend yourself. I know Monae and she would have jumped you if you didn't. I for one am proud of you, ma, and so is my whole family. Monae wanted trouble and she got it. I know she won't even look at you sideways after that," I laughed and squeezed her hand.

We pulled on a street a block from Honey's apartment, so I decided to just ask her and get it over with.

"Honey, I've been thinking, I know you just got your apartment and it's only been just over a month with us but, I love having you around and being with you. So, I guess I'm asking you if you would move in with me," I asked but she didn't answer.

I turned to look at her but she wasn't looking at me and I don't think she even heard me. Her focus was on something else and then I saw tears start to fall. I stopped the car when I saw what she was looking at.

"What the fuck?!"

# Chapter Five

*Honey*

**Earlier that day**

It felt so good punching Monae in the throat. In the words of Tasha, the bitch was testing my gangsta. I may not be from the streets, but don't get shit twisted my ass could fight. My momma was worried about me being a girl, and being her only child living in Chicago. Although I grew up away from the projects, bullies weren't only in the projects. Because I was a pretty girl, there were boys who liked me and the girls who wanted them, found themselves having an attitude wanting to fight me.

My momma made me go to karate classes when I was growing up. While other little girls were doing ballet and dancing, I was learning how to defend myself and kick ass. There wasn't a bitch who had beaten me yet. Most times it didn't even end up being a fight once I gave them a single punch to the throat. But let's not forget, my best friends were a bunch of gangsta, dysfunctional motherfuckers who whooped ass for fun!

I had been at Ky-mani's house for a few days now. I liked being with him, and as soon as he was about to take me back home, we decide that one more day wouldn't hurt. And one day turned into two, but tonight I was definitely going home because I didn't want him to think I was a clingy person; because I was far from that, but I couldn't help wanting to be near him.

I think the upside to it was that he felt the same way!

I couldn't wait to get into work and tell the girls what happened. I gave Ky-mani a long, deep kiss as I climbed out of his car. My car had been home since he picked me up three days ago, so he had been taking me to work and picking me up, which he said he liked to do. But no matter what, I was going home today.

We still hadn't slept together yet although we both wanted to. I guess when the moment was right, we would both know it.

As soon as I walked into my office, I went looking for Tasha and Kelis. I found them in the canteen with Tasha stuffing her face as usual.

"Come to my office, I need to give you two some jokes," I said and Tasha got up and ran ahead of us. Crazy

70

bitch.

Kelis and I just shook our heads and followed Tasha.

"Come on tell me. Did you fuck, Ky-mani?" Tasha asked, bouncing up and down.

"Bitch, I swear all you think about is dick or food," I said and laughed.

"Well is there anything else that's better than both?" she said. I actually had to think and she was right, there was nothing. We laughed.

"Anyway, yesterday Ky-mani calls me and said how he's got to leave work and get his kids because Monae didn't pick them up, and left them at school. I was free so I told him I would get them and bring them to her when she got home. Everything was going okay until the bitch arrived at the mall with two friends, trying to fight me," I laughed.

"Shut the fuck up. Why didn't you call me? I would have fucked that bitch up!" Tasha said and I laughed.

"Oh hell no, Honey, what did you do?" Kelis asked and I went quiet.

"I punched that bitch straight in her throat," I said and they fell out laughing.

They were both holding their stomachs as they laughed uncontrollably. "Oh shit, Honey. That's too funny," Tasha laughed.

"Good, I don't feel sorry for the bitch. What did Ky-mani say?" Kelis asked.

"He was happy. He said if it was him or if he was there, he would have shot her ass," I said and we all laughed again.

"And I believe him too," Kelis said.

"Trifling bitch. I bet she won't fuck with you again," Tasha laughed.

"Shit, that bitch tried to test my gangsta!" I said and Tasha dapped me up.

"Wait until Sydney hears this shit. Why did she have to be on leave today?" Tasha sucked her teeth.

"Speaking of Sydney, she just emailed us," I said, scanning through my emails.

"Oh yeah, what she say?" Tasha asked as her and Kelis come over by me to see the computer screen.

*Sydney: what's up bitches missing me :)*

*Me: hell no bitch lol.*

*Sydney: lying bitches. So, what's good? What y'all up to?*

*Me: just chatting about me punching Ky-mani's b momma in the throat. The bitch came to the mall with two friends trying to jump me, can you believe that shit?*

72

*Sydney: oh man why couldn't I be there. You know I haven't fought anyone in a hot minute lol.*

I laughed at Sydney, but I know she was dead ass serious.

"Ask her what's she doing," Tasha said and I nodded my head.

*Me: so, what you up to? Missing us on your off day?*

*Sydney: I'm just here with Tyron's ass. Nigga is behind me thinking he doing shit to my pussy all sweating and shit. But I can't feel a fucking thing.*

I had to take a back seat for a minute; did I just read what I thought I did?

"Yo girls, read this for me," I said, moving out of the way so they could get to my computer screen.

Kelis and Tasha looked at each other and screamed laughing. They were laughing so much they couldn't even talk.

"Yo, is this bitch fucking and emailing us?" Tasha laughed until tears came. So, I did read it right. I swear Sydney was the worst.

*Me: Sydney, are you fucking a nigga and emailing us???*

*Sydney: Yeah. This nigga ain't doing shit, and I had things to do. I'm bent over the bed so I thought I would check my*

73

*emails and email you bitches.*

We read it and laughed our asses off. This bitch had no goddamn chill I swear.

*Sydney: oh shit this nigga gone fall asleep. Tell Tasha to call me in ten and pretend to be my boss. This nigga needs to get out.*

I showed Tasha the message but I couldn't even reply because I was scared of what her crazy ass might tell me next.

"So you give Law the goodies yet?" Kelis asked and I shook my head.

"Why? What are you waiting for? Tasha asked.

"I don't know. I'm afraid for some reason. Plus, every time we touch each other he tells me he promises not to penetrate me, so I don't think he's ready to either. And I don't want to look like an eager bitch by telling him to take it," I explained.

"What are you scared of?" Tasha asked.

"Well for one of it hurting," I said and they laughed at me.

"But also of things changing. We are so happy and everything is going great, what if afterwards things change?"

"I don't see how Honey and if anything, it should bring y'all closer together," Tasha said and I nodded my head.

"How was meeting his family?" Kelis asked. I completely forgot to tell them about it.

"Oh, it was good. His momma, Doreen, is lovely; and his two sisters, Toya and Nevaeh, are cool. They wanted to beat up Monae for me," I laughed.

"I even met Ricky's momma, Ruth, and her husband, Marco. But he wasn't so keen on me, but Ky-mani said he's always cautious about new people coming around his family, especially the women. Apparently, Ky-mani hasn't been known to mess with the nicest girls," I said putting it nicely but in plain English; he fucked with bitch ass, ghetto hoes.

We chatted for a few more minutes before they left to start work.

I didn't have many clients to meet up with, but I had a bit of paperwork to finalize, so I started on that. The receptionist, Julie, came in and interrupted me.

"Sorry, Miss Honey, there's a client in the reception area who was supposed to meet with Mr. Talbi but he called in sick. This appointment wasn't in the books; otherwise I would have canceled it. But I was just wondering if you weren't too busy, could you meet with him please?" she asked in a panicked state. I knew from her reaction that the

75

client must have been acting a damn fool, so I agreed to help her out.

"Send him in. What's his name?"

"Leeroy James," she said, thanking me and rushing out.

I put my file away and got myself ready to meet with this client. He better not be on no bullshit because I was ready to send his ass out. I had a zero- bullshit tolerance policy.

There was a knock at the door. "Come in," I said and stood to my feet to greet this client.

In walked a middle height, slim man with lots of hair pushed under a fitted Nike cap. He had on a pair of black True Religion jeans, black Timberlands, and a white t-shirt. He shook my hand and adjusted his cap on his head.

"How can I help you?"

"I'm interested in buying some property and would like to know what my accounts are looking like so I can know if I can make that thought a reality," he said, smiling at me.

I logged onto the accounting section of our systems and then handed him the tablet so he could enter his account information.

"Thank you," I said, when he handed the tablet over to me.

"Here is a review of your accountants, Mr. James," I said and handed him a printout.

He looked over it for a few minutes before looking up at me.

"I guess I'm going to be a new resident. Do you know anyone you could recommend to show me around town?" he said.

"No sorry, I wouldn't."

"Well, how about you?" he said, running his hand across his bottom lip.

"I'm sorry, I have a boyfriend," I said and he smiled.

"Ok but I have a lot of money, ma. I can give you anything your little pretty ass desires," he said and I laughed.

"Mr. James, I have a boyfriend who takes care of all my needs and more. But I'm sure you have eyes and see me sitting her in an Armani suit and Giuseppes on my feet, so I don't run chase money. So please don't confuse me for a money hungry thot because I'm not," I said and folded my arms across my chest.

"I see I'm dealing with a queen so please let me apologize for my insinuation, I just meant I could look after you, ma. You're just so beautiful. I'm not a cocky dude but I know how I look," he said and I leaned forward so he would catch what I was about to say.

"You've not seen my nigga, Mr. James, and I can assure you, ain't no nigga alive who looks like him. He's life itself and I would be a damn fool to walk away from a god like that. Trust and believe my nigga has it like that and more," I smiled at him.

"Damn I believe you, ma. Your dude is a lucky nigga. Pardon, my French but bitches ain't loyal; but I saw the passion in your eyes when you spoke about him. I wish I had a girl like you who loved me like you love your dude," he said, standing to his feet.

"Pleasure doing business with you,- Honey," he said, reading my plaque.

"If you ever change your mind, here is my business card," he said, trying to hand it to me but I didn't take it.

"I'm good; I won't ever change my mind."

"Homeboy got it like that?"

"You have no idea," I said, smiling to myself. He finally admitted defeat and left my office.

I finished up my work for the rest of the day until it was time to meet Ky-mani.

He texted me when he was outside, so I gathered up my belongings and went out to meet him.

My girls and I strolled out of the building chatting and giggling.

"What's up, ladies? How y'all doing?" Ky-mani asked Tasha and Kelis.

"Good. How are you doing?" Tasha asked him.

"Better now," he said, looking at me and making me blush. Like I said, ain't no one like my man.

"Ohhh go, Ky-mani.," they both said and laughed.

"See y'all tomorrow," I said, hugging them and climbing into Ky-mani's car.

"What's good, ma?" he asked and kissed me.

"I'm good, how was your day?" I asked him as he drove away.

"It was good baby, thanks. And guess what, my cousin came down after being released from jail," he smiled and I rubbed his hand.

"I'll let you meet him soon," he said and I nodded. "So how was your day?"

"It was good. But I had a client hit on me today, though. The first time that's ever happened. I sent him on his way," I said and he went quiet.

"That's the first time that's ever happened?" he asked me.

"Yeah, that's never happened before."

"Wow, I'm surprised because you're so beautiful; even I wanted to talk to you when I first saw you."

"Well, most of my clients are women or married

79

men," I said and he nodded.

As we got closer to my apartment, Ky-mani grew quiet and I could see he was thinking deeply about something.

"Are you upset with me or something Ky-mani?"

"Oh no, Honey, not at all. I was just thinking about something."

"Ok, something troubling you?"

"No, but let me ask you something. I know we have only been together for a little over a month, but you make me happy, Honey, and I just love being around you. Maybe I'm moving too fast but it just feels so right, Honey. These last few days having you around has been the best time. I love sleeping next to you and waking up next to you. I guess I should just spit it out. I just want to know if you would move in with me?" he said as he turned onto my road.

But the sight before me made me unable to talk. I was in shock. My eyes tried to make sense of what I was seeing. Blue lights flashed around me causing the tears that formed to burn as they poured out.

"Oh my God!" I screamed out.

Ky-mani stopped the car and I climbed out slowly. There were people standing by, paramedics running

80

around and firefighters fighting to put the flames out in my apartment! My apartment was on fire and so was my car. I looked around and realized that my apartment was the only one in flames. It was so big that it completely covered what was once my apartment and I could feel the heat burning my face from where I stood.

"Oh my God, there she is!" I heard my elderly neighbor, Mrs. Jones, scream out. Cops, firefighters, and paramedics rushed over to me with Mrs. Jones. She wrapped her arms around me and cried sourly on my shoulder.

"I thought you were in there, Honey," she cried.

"Ma'am are you ok? Where have you been?" a cop asked me, but I was unable to speak.

Ky-mani came over and answered their questions for me.

My heart sank as my home disappeared. I didn't care about my car; there wasn't anything but a few CDs in there and some other unimportant junk. But my home had everything I ever worked for and owned in there. Things my momma gave me, photos of my family members, items I was given by my grandfather before he died. Things that I could never replace were all gone.

I dropped to the ground on my knees. Ky-mani grabbed me and picked me up. My whole world got turned upside

81

down. How could this have happened?

"Honey!" Ky-mani called me and I looked up at him. "Did you hear what the cop said? Someone started this fire by throwing a petrol bomb through your window," he said, catching my attention.

Someone tried to kill me?!

I dropped my head on his shoulder and cried my eyes out. The cop allowed us to leave, so he carried me to his car and gently put me in. He ran around to the other side and climbed in. "Baby?" he said but I continued to cry.

Someone actually tried to kill me?!

He leaned over me and buckled my seatbelt for me. He quickly started the car and drove me to his house.

I was now homeless with no clothes, no belongings, nothing but what I had on my back and in my purse. My identification was all in the apartment; documents, trust fund information, bank details, everything.

The storm had finally hit but little did I know; it was just the beginning.

# Chapter Six

*Law*

I couldn't believe that Honey's apartment was gone! Somebody purposely set it on fire. The fear that hit me when the cop I knew explained what the neighbors saw, was indescribable. It wasn't a case of randomness; Honey was the target! It was no coincidence that her car and apartment were targeted. Whoever did it thought she was home because of her car being out front.

God knows if I hadn't picked her up today, she would have gone home and I could be dealing with her death.

It pained me to see my beautiful queen in such a state. I had never seen her cry until then. The way she collapsed to the ground; I knew she was defeated. I couldn't shake the tingling in my mind that this happened because of me!

Honey was new to this town; no one knew her, for her to be the target, so that only left me. And that would mean, I had someone at my head and they wanted to break me by getting rid of Honey.

I wanted her to stay with me but not like this. But all I

83

knew was, I was glad that she would be staying with me. All
of my security staff was going to be on high alert. I was
doubling the presence around my family and camp. Whoever
did this needed to be found and quick.

When I got home with Honey, she was still in shock
staring into space. I carried her out of the car and into the
house. She clung to me tightly as I carried her up the stairs. I
went straight into the bathroom and sat on the edge of the
bathtub. I ran the water and stripped her out of her clothes as
the bathtub filled.

When it was full, I gently placed her in it.

I picked up her clothes and went to put them in the
hamper.

It broke my heart that the only clothes she owned I had
just taken off, excluding a few items in my hamper from the
last couple of days that she spent with me. I heard her start
crying again and it burned my heart. My baby was broken
and I didn't know how to fix things.

I grabbed a t-shirt from my dresser and laid it out on
the bed. In Honey's drawer that she used when she stayed
over, I found a pair of panties and threw that on the bed too.

I went into the bathroom and she was sitting covering
her eyes.

"Everything I owned is gone. Why would somebody

do that? Things my grandpa gave me; photos of him, letters, his ashes, all my furniture…it's all gone," she said.

I kissed her tears and pulled her into my arms. I grabbed the washcloth and started to wash her down.

When I was done, I wrapped the towel around her and carried her out. I dried her body and pulled on the clothes that I laid out.

I took off my wet clothes and climbed into bed with her. I held her tight until she fell asleep.

My mind was doing overtime; I couldn't even think straight.

I gently climbed out of bed so I wouldn't wake her and pulled on some clothes.

I checked the monitors and made sure the guards were patrolling. Usually, I would have one on site sitting in the office because like I said I was retired from these streets. And it had been over two years since anybody was at me like that to warrant security but all of that changed today.

I went into my office and texted my crew 911!

Thirty minutes later and my office was full with my most loyal little niggas and my crew heads: KY, Drake, Ricky, and now Cameron.

85

I sat at the head of the table and puffed on a blunt. Everyone sat with their eyes on me waiting for me to speak. It had been so long since I called a meeting like this, so I knew that they knew some shit was going on.

I had been retired for a year but I would gladly come out over Honey. She was my life and my livelihood and anybody who fucked with her, signed themselves a death warrant.

"I called y'all here tonight because somebody took a shot at Honey," I said.

"Cuz, is she ok?" Ricky asked.

"She's good. She's upstairs asleep but some motherfucker blew up her house today hoping that she was in it. They took a shot at my queen and for that it's unforgivable," I said and puffed on the blunt.

"I want y'all eyes and ears out there. I wanna know who and I wanna know why. And then I want that motherfucker so I can end their life with my bare hands!" I spat thumping my fists down on the table.

"Beef up on security and watch your asses. Y'all slip and you slide. I won't tolerate slacking because I'll kill you myself before I let your fuck up be the end of me or Honey," I let them know. Law was officially out of retirement until the people behind this paid.

At the end of the meeting, my niggas stayed back and drank with me. My head was full of what ifs and I needed to drown them out. They became a distant memory after half a bottle of Hennessy. After they left, I took off my clothes and climbed in bed with my woman.

Morning came and Honey was still fast asleep curled into a ball. My baby was sad and hurting. I looked around the room and I didn't even have a pair of bedroom slippers to put on her feet. How do you go from having everything you could ever need to three dresses, one top, one skirt, three bras, four panties, and a nightshirt? That was all that Honey had left.

I picked up her phone and wrote some numbers down and went into my office to make some calls. I managed to pull some strings and get what I needed to happen. I went upstairs to handle my personal hygiene before they arrived. Honey was still asleep. Ma tossed and turned the whole night, so I could understand why she was so tired.

The doorbell rang as I stood watching her sleep. I stroked her face gently and went to answer the door.

"Thank you, ladies, for coming," I said as I greeted

Tasha, Kelis, Sydney, Toya, and Nevaeh.

I put my finger up to indicate not to talk and led them to my office.

"Ky-mani, what happened to Honey?" Tasha said as soon as I closed the office door.

"Someone blew up her house and her car yesterday," I said. They all went hysterical and started speaking at once.

"Ladies, she's ok; she's upstairs safe and asleep. She was with me and not at home," I said, trying to calm them down.

"Who did that?" Kelis asked.

"I do not know nor do I know why," I confessed. They all started talking again.

"Ladies, please," I said loudly and they sat quietly.

"Ok, I asked you all here for two reasons. One, as you can imagine everything Honey owned was in that house. So, I was wondering since y'all know her the best," I said, pointing to her friends, "I thought that maybe y'all could go to the mall and buy anything and everything you know Honey had or would like," I said, looking at them.

"Ah shit, shopping! Yeah, baby," Tasha said and I laughed.

"Yeah, in that case, I'm not giving your happy ass the credit card," I said and everyone laughed.

"Right, now I called you two here to go and get Honey a new car. I want it decked out in the best equipment and customized with Honey's initials all over and in whatever her favorite color is."

"Pink," her friends called out.

"Thanks y'all," I smiled.

"Is that cool with y'all? It's just that I don't want Honey waking up to an empty house if I was to do it."

"Yeah, that's cool. Anything for our girl," Sydney said and her friends nodded to agree.

"Bro you know we down, we care for Honey too," Nevaeh said.

"I don't care the price so don't look at that. If Honey had it or would like it, then I want it ok?" I said, handing a black card to Kelis as she was closest to me and one to Nevaeh as she was the eldest.

"Don't worry about pin numbers. My bank will text me alerts and as long as I don't respond, it will go through. Just tap that sucker on the readers. Y'all good."

"And the second part is helping to cheer up Honey. My baby has been so down since it happened and this isn't like her. I know she's got me but I also know sometimes laughter is the quickest healer. And I know how females like to be gossiping and cracking jokes and shit; I've seen y'all Facebook pages," I said and laughed.

I was happy to see that they all agreed with my plans and rushed out of there to get it done. Me being me, I was handy for this situation because once I called their bosses and school and explained what happened and who I was, instantly they were given a free day. I even got Honey a week off of work so she could have some time for herself.

As soon as the girls left, security called to say someone was down at the gate causing trouble, and there was only person I knew who could fuck the security off to the point that they wanted to shoot them, and that was Monae.

I grabbed my keys and rushed down to the gate. Tasha, Kelis, and Sydney had surrounded the bitch looking like they wanted to beat her ass. I should have let them but I just wanted Monae's ass gone off of my property.

"Ladies, it's all good I got this," I said. They stared her down and made sure to bump her something hard, as they passed. They kept their mean mugs focused on her as they jumped into Kelis' car and drove off.

"Law, who were those women? You got bitches out here trying to jump me?"

"What's wrong with three against one? Isn't that your style?" I said and she rolled her eyes.

"Didn't I tell your ass not to come back over here? You don't even have my kids so you definitely shouldn't be back over here," I said.

"Law, you were serious about that?" she asked wide eyed.

"Of course, Monae. I was dead ass serious as my security has already shown your ass."

"I just came to talk to you and apologize about the mix up with the kids," she said and I started to laugh.

"There wasn't no mix-up. Clearly, you were trying to play a game and your ass got caught out. One minute you helping your grandma somewhere and couldn't get to the kids' school in time and the next, you in the mall five minutes after I tell you Honey is there with the kids. And the joke of it all was that you had to pass the kids' school to get to the mall."

"Okay you're right; but I was just trying to annoy you after you put me out."

"Damn right I put you out. Your ass wasn't supposed to be here in the first place. Look Monae, ain't nothing else to say. I meant what I said about coming back here when I want to see the kids., I will call you and then pick them up myself. So, don't turn up here no more to our house," I said.

"What you mean our house?"

"Honey lives here now. So, you don't have the right to show up on her property," I said.

The last thing I needed was Monae showing up here when she felt like it, making Honey believe that's what she did before.

91

She just stood there with her mouth opened looking at me. "Bye Monae," I said and walked away.

When I got back into the house, I heard Honey upstairs walking about. I walked into the room to I find her pacing our bedroom floor, talking and crying to someone on the phone.

When she turned and saw me, she smiled through her tears at me and went back to pacing the floor.

"I know, Momma," she said and sniffed.

I was yet to meet or talk to her momma. Honey said she told her about me but I didn't know what exactly. Did she tell her about Ky-mani or Law? I could see Honey getting more upset by the minute, so I sat on the bed and signaled for her to come over onto my lap.

She did and I put my hand on the phone and she handed it to me. "Good morning, Miss Johnson," I said.

"Oh, Ky-mani, good morning, son. Thank you so much for being there for my daughter and taking care of her. She told me how you stepped in and took her in and nurtured her when she was in such a state. I can't help thinking that if she hadn't met you or wasn't with you last night, I would have lost my baby," she sniffed and I realized she was crying too.

"Miss Johnson, I know I haven't met you yet and it would have been much better if I did before Honey came to live with me. But I promise you with everything in me that I

92

love your daughter, ma'am, and I will look after her and protect her until my last breath," I said, trying to comfort her.

"I know baby, I know. She's down now because she loved her grandfather. They had a special bond and everything she had regarding him was in that house. Be strong for the both of you, ok son and everything else will work out."

"Yes, ma'am."

"Oh and, Ky-mani, just one thing. Please let me at least meet you before you give her a baby," she laughed.

"Don't worry, Miss Johnson, it's not that kind of relationship at the moment." I know it's not something a mother needed to hear, but at the same time she did. I didn't want her thinking I was there dicking her daughter down and impregnating her in her time of stress. Even though, I wanted to be dicking her down and eventually get her pregnant.

Hey, I'm a thug, not a liar.

But I liked how she said some more grandbabies because that meant she knew about my kids and accepted them.

"I know and that's why I love you. Nowadays, no man who would do that and that is why I trust you with my baby. Please make sure she leaves the room and eats, Ky-mani."

"I will, ma'am."

93

"Oh, son, don't call me ma'am, I ain't old like that," she laughed. "And don't call me Miss Johnson either. I'm Patrice, Momma P, Momma, whichever you feel happy calling me. You're my family now," she said and I smiled.

"Ok, Momma P," I smiled and hugged Honey even tighter.

"Kiss my baby for me and y'all look after each other and no matter what, keep the love Ky-mani because love can conquer all," she said.

I kissed Honey like she wanted me to and ended my call with her. "I'm sorry, baby," I whispered and stroked her face softly.

"I'm ok, babe, thank you. It's just that I have nothing to remember him by because it's all gone now," she said lowly.

"You do, baby, he's right here," I said, placing a hand on her heart.

I took her downstairs and I cooked breakfast for her. She was trying to smile but I could see her pain. She was still so beautiful but I could see the anger in her eyes. She wanted to know who did it as much as I did.

She sat on the couch staring at the TV but not really watching it. I smiled because Tasha had texted to say they were on the way back as well as my sisters. The new clothes and car may not let her forget her pain, but it would be two things she wouldn't have to worry about.

The doorbell rang and she looked up at me wondering who it was, but I just smiled and pulled open the door.

She started laughing when she saw the girls rush in. "Bitches," she shouted at them and they all hugged and laughed. My sisters went over to her and kissed and hugged her too. I sat back on the couch looking at them and feeling satisfied.

They all started chatting and laughing. I knew this was what she needed.

Toya came over and headed me a pair of keys and winked at me.

I mouthed thank you and approached Honey.

"Come here, baby," I said and pulled her up to her feet and led her outside. I was just as surprised as Honey when I saw my sisters got her a black on black Range Rover that matched mine.

"Oh my god, Ky-mani! You didn't," she said, looking at me.

"I sure did, momma," I said and she tiptoed and kissed me.

"You do too much for me already, Ky-mani. I didn't want you to have to do this," she said, looking into my eyes.

"I didn't do it because I had to; I did it because I wanted to. I meant it when I told your momma that I love you," I said.

"I love you too, Ky-mani," she said, hugging on to

95

me.

I pulled her over to her new car and handed her the keys. When she opened it, it was filled with bags of clothes and shoes.

"What?" she asked and started laughing.

"Now how am I gonna buy you a car but leave you naked?" I said and she laughed.

The girls grabbed the bags so she could look at the inside of the Range Rover.

It was all black and pink with leather interior and her name written in fancy pink letters on the upholstery. That usually took a few weeks to be done but because it was for me, it was done in hours.

I stood and watched as she smiled and talked with the girls.

It was good to see her talking and smiling. Her friends and my sisters were nice distractions for her.

Now all I need to do was find out who took her smile away. I hope they were ready because Law was hitting the town!

# Chapter Seven

*Honey*

When I saw my house in flames I was crushed. I worked my ass off to buy the things that I owned. Yes, my family came from money and I had a trust fund set up by my grandpa, but I wanted to work for my things just like my momma did. So, I got a job when I was seventeen to save up and take care of myself.

I then got myself a little apartment and enrolled in school. I continued to study and work until I met Jerome. I moved in with him and I continued to work my ass off; finished school, and got a well-paying job. Then we bought our house together. When my grandpa died, he left me an inheritance. I put that in my savings account but continued to work, because I liked knowing I worked for my money and wasn't given it on a platter. Sure, I could have easily lived off my family's money but there's no joy or satisfaction in that.

When I moved into my own apartment after leaving

97

Jerome, I purchased that apartment with my hard-earned savings that I accumulated over the years.

To have done all that and in a single night lose it all, was beyond soul crushing. Losing things my grandpa gave me hurt beyond words. They were irreplaceable things; birthday cards, letters, dolls he gave me as a child, photos of me and him together, souvenirs he gave me when he traveled, clothing, blankets, and so much more. Twenty-two years I spent with him as he died last year. That's years of items that

I would never be able to replace, including his ashes. My grandma couldn't bear having them in her house after he died, so I took them with me. And now he and all my memories of him were gone.

Why would someone do that and on purpose? I heard the officer tell Ky-mani it was a targeted attack, but all I kept thinking was did they hope I was there or were they just targeting my belongings? That I did not know.

Ky-mani had been so good to me; he was my strength in all of this. I was glad he was asking me to move in with him at that time, otherwise, I would have felt like I was taking over and I didn't want him to feel obligated to let me move in. But fate had it that he asked me on that day.

I cried every time I thought of my grandpa. I felt so bad for Ky-mani because he was left with a depressed version of Honey but he was my rock. He made me feel like it was okay to be sad and never lost his temper with me.

I couldn't believe he bought me a whole new wardrobe of clothes and a new car. I didn't want him to have to do that, but I was grateful. I still had money in my savings account, my checking account, and my job; but I had no ID to get money from the bank and my credit cards only allowed so much to be taken. So, I wouldn't have been able to buy a new car and clothes on just my credit card like that.

My momma was so stressed out when I told her what happened, but when I told her all that Ky-mani had done for me, she was happy. Even though they hadn't met in person, she liked him very much for me from the little that I told her. My momma was my best friend so I could talk to her about anything.

I told her about his kids and she was so accepting and supportive, especially because he had told me on our first date. She loved that he was so honest with me.

I even told her that we hadn't had sex yet. She said he was definitely a keeper! He could do no wrong in her eyes and I was glad she liked him. She didn't dislike Jerome but she did take a while to warm to him; maybe because we were young and I had lost my virginity to him, but in the end, she hated him for what he did.

I can't believe he was still calling her up until recently, even after Ky-mani warned him to leave me alone. He actually called my momma and left a message saying how I left him for a gangsta. I'm glad she knew why I really left and that he wasn't shit. She blocked his number, but he just uses another phone to call her.

I should tell Ky-mani, but my momma said not to.

Ky-mani was the best. He arranged for my girls and his sisters to come and surprise me. It was nice to have them around to distract me from what had happened.

He went off into his office to work and left us alone, so I grabbed some drinks and went out into the garden to sit around the pool.

"So I heard y'all wanted to fight Monae too?" Sydney said to Ky-mani's sisters.

"Hell yeah, I hate that bitch. I always wanted to pop on her ass but just because of the kids I didn't. She's a sneaky, pussy bitch, because I know my brother would never fuck her and get her pregnant on purpose. He was adamant that he never fucked her without a condom and I believe him," Toya said.

"Yeah, he said he didn't," I admitted.

"My brother isn't a liar, Honey. I know that thot did something to trap him on purpose. I'm not surprised, though; she is known around town as the bitch who cried pregnancy," Toya laughed.

"Cried pregnancy?" I asked confused.

"Oh, y'all don't know? I keep forgetting you're not from this town. Monae always fucked around with niggas with money. She started messing around with some pro ballers and when they had enough, she claimed she was pregnant, but that bitch was lying."

"Then all of a sudden, Ky-mani is the new prince of the town and started rising in the streets. Money was flowing through his hands and he was building up the town. Next thing you know, he fucks her twice with a condom and the bitch is pregnant. Fuck outta here," Toya vented.

Wow, I thought Ky-mani complained about Monae to maybe make himself look like he had no interest in her. But listening to Toya, I see it's not just Ky-mani, something is not right with that woman.

"Yeah but who can trust a woman who fucked her momma's boyfriend," Nevaeh said.

My girls and I looked at each other and then back at them. Did I just hear, right?

"What you say, Nevaeh?" Tasha asked.

"Yeah you heard right. This nasty ass bitch fucked her momma's boyfriend and then moved in with him. She got pregnant for him many times, but had abortions each time. But yet, she's quick to have my brother's kids," Toya said and shook her head.

"Her momma went all over town telling this bitch's secrets. I don't even think she knows," Nevaeh laughed and so did we.

*Who fucks their momma's man?*

"So what happened to the boyfriend?" I asked.

"She left him when she met Ky-mani. That bitch had a motive towards my brother from the beginning. She's just jealous of you, Honey, because she will never be you or have what you have," Toya said and Nevaeh nodded her head.

"That bitch is crazy," Sydney said, laughing.

"Talking about crazy, did your ass really email us when you were fucking somebody?" Tasha asked and we all fell out laughing.

"Oh God; forgive my friend please, girls. She's as mad as they come," I said apologizing for Sydney because I knew nothing good was going to come out of this conversation.

Toya and Nevaeh laughed. Their asses couldn't wait to hear this shit. My ass was scared every time she spoke because I never knew what shit would come out of it!

"Ignore, Honey. But I sure was. I had shit to do. That nigga wasn't hitting shit; all breaking a fucking sweat like he working something. I had to turn my back to him during fucking because he was sweating like hell and I didn't want any of his craziness to drop in my eye," Sydney said and we chocked on our sodas laughing at her.

"So what happened with that guy from your building?" I asked and giggled. Every time I saw him, I remembered that dick breaking dream Sydney had about him.

"That nigga right there," she started and shook her head.

"This nigga was all up in my face, flirting, and shit; making it his business to fuck with me whenever he saw me, so I told him to come over. This retarded nigga found himself trying to play with my titties over my clothes and then asks me if I discharged?" she said.

"What the fuck? Did he mean cum?" I said, trying hard not to laugh.

"Yeah! Like who cums from a nigga playing with their clothes?" she said and I shook my head.

"I told his ass that I was married and my husband was coming home. He ran up out of there with his stupid black ass. Talking about did you discharge? It's cum, nigga," she scoffed and we laughed at her.

"Talking about sex," Tasha started and I rolled my eyes hard at her because I knew what was coming next.

"You still haven't given Ky-mani some of yo cookies?" she whispered and the girls giggled.

"Oh, here it goes," I said, sucking my teeth.

"Wait, Honey, you and my brother haven't done it?" Nevaeh said, causing the others to laugh at her choice of words.

"No, not yet," I said and picked up my drink to hide my face in.

"Oh, Honey, he's feeling you hard because he would never do that," Toya said, smiling.

"So, not trying to be in your business, sis. But don't you want to?" she asked me.

"Oh please, this bitch dying to drop that pussy on him, don't make her fool you," Tasha screeched and we all laughed.

"No, it's just that he said when we were both ready we would know," I said and they nodded their heads.

The truth is I was ready, but I didn't want to beg him to or come on strong, leading him to think I was acting like a thot; so I would wait until he wanted it. It's not like I could hide it from him; I got dressed in front of him, we showered together, and we would fool around with him sucking the life out of me, but he just never tried or even asked if he could.

He always said he wouldn't penetrate me and he never did.

Maybe he just wasn't ready!

We sat and chatted for some time until they all left. I went to go check on Ky-mani and found him asleep on his office couch. He had been so good to me and worrying about me, so I'm not surprised that he was tired with all that he did today; getting me a new car, clothes, and organizing my friends to come over. He was the best.

I decided to let him sleep and cook him some dinner. I decided to whip up some Mac and Cheese, lamb chops, baby potatoes, and corn. As that was cooking, I unloaded my car.

I was in awe as I packed away pretty much the same clothes I had just lost and a few new items. He had cleared one side of his walk-in closet for me to use.

It felt weird sharing a home with Ky-mani, but it felt good at the same time. I didn't want to jinx anything, but as soon as I could, I was going to look for another apartment. I didn't want to make him feel bombarded and overcrowded by me. I don't think he has lived with a woman before, and although this was what he wanted, I knew first hand that being with someone and living with them was completely different.

The last thing I wanted was for him to realize that, and I had nowhere else to go. For the most part, I will enjoy it like he wants me to. I can see he's happy about it… But it's only been one night!

Once I was finished unpacking everything, I went down to wake him up.

He was sleeping so peacefully. He was so beautiful with the most perfect features ever. His hair was pulled back in a ponytail. His hair was neatly lined with precision all the way around his hairline and down to his beard. His thin mustache was sharp and neat. He had on a wife beater and basketball shorts.

He looked so good; I could eat him up.

His tattoos that covered his sleeve were so beautiful. He was the perfect specimen of a man, and I could see why Monae went crazy over him. Shit, I probably would too.

I stood over him and ran my hand gently over his tattoos and his eyes popped open.

"Hello, my beautiful," he smiled and picked up my hand

to kiss it.

"Hello, baby," I smiled.

He sat up and pulled me down onto his lap. "Everybody gone?" he asked and I nodded my head.

"Yo, my trifling sisters didn't even come to tell me bye," he groaned and I laughed.

"They did tell me to tell you bye," I smiled. He shook his head.

"Let's go, I made you some dinner," I kissed him and pulled him up off the couch and led him to the kitchen.

I sat him down at the table and fixed him a plate.

"Wow, ma, when did you cook this?" he asked, staring at his plate.

"When you were sleeping; I thought you would be hungry when you woke up."

He pulled me close and gave me a deep, passionate kiss.

"I don't know what I did to deserve you but I'm grateful you're in my life," he kissed me again.

"No, it's me who is grateful. I was devastated and a mess but you were my rock. You went above and beyond for me and I'm blessed to have found you," I hugged onto him tightly.

In such a short span of time, I had fallen in love with this man. He was so gentle, thoughtful and kind towards me. I couldn't pick or ask for a better man.

We ate dinner and spoke about life and our next steps. I loved being in his presence, but I just couldn't help but feel like things wouldn't remain like this!

After he cleared away our plates, he ran a hot bath. He pulled me playfully into the bathroom and removed my clothes. He picked me up and put me into the bath. I just loved how strong he was and how he picked me up so easily. I felt so safe in his arms.

He pulled off his clothes. He was so magnificently made and so well endowed. He must have been about twelve inches long and thick as hell. As much as I wanted nothing more than to feel him inside of me, I was petrified.

He caught me looking and chuckled as he climbed in the bath. He grabbed a washcloth and started to wash my body down. When he was done, I did the same to him.

As soon as my hand touched him, he was hard as a rock. He laughed and stroked my face gently.

He lifted me up and placed me on the edge of the bath. He opened my legs, parted my pussy, and pushed his head deeply between my thighs. I had to grip onto the side of the bathtub as he devoured my pussy.

"I just love the way you smell and taste, Honey. So,

sweet," he whispered and flicked his tongue back and forth against me.

He pulled me closer into his mouth until he was nose deep into me. He sucked, nibbled, and flicked my clit causing my body to shake uncontrollably. He inserted a finger as he continued to suck hard on me. I opened my legs wider to let him in and also so if he wanted to give me the dick finally, he could.

But a few seconds later, I came long, hard and loudly. He continued to kiss and lick me, mopping up all my juices.

"That's my baby," he said, kissing my lips before pulling me out of the bath with him. We dried each other like an old married couple. He pulled on boxers and I pulled on panties and a bra. I went to pull on a night shirt but he pulled it out of my hand.

"You don't need clothes, baby," he smiled.

He laid down and I climbed in bed onto his chest. He kissed the top of my head before wrapping his arms around me.

I felt like I was being blatant when I opened my legs the way I did. I wanted to tell him to take me but maybe like I said – he wasn't ready.

# Chapter Eight

## *Monae*

When I saw Honey's apartment in flames I wished I had thought of that myself. I got her address from her driver's license when she was at Law's house that weekend she met my kids. She was so busy fucking my man that she left her purse in the kitchen.

I was pissed when I saw it because this bitch was only twenty-three!

I wrote her address down but I wasn't sure what I was going to do with it until that day in the mall when she punched my ass. Law didn't even care; it was like he was proud of her for hitting me.

I saw red and I thought I would sneak into that bitch's apartment and slice her throat in her sleep, but I guess someone beat me to it and had a better idea.

I rode home with a smile on my face. I got up early and with pep in my step.

"Good morning, mommy's babies, did y'all sleep well?" I smiled and kissed the kids. I had made them blueberry pancakes and a fruit salad. I sang and danced around the kitchen.

"Mommy, you're happy," Chyna said smiling.

She wasn't lying because I truly was. I couldn't remember the last time I was so happy like this around the house. The only time I was happy was when I was seeing Law.

"Yeah, mommy is going to get your daddy and we are going to be a family

finally," I smiled.

"Now hurry up and eat before we are late for school," I said as I danced my ass out of the kitchen to get dressed.

I pulled on a tight white maxi dress and white sandals. I straightened my weave and brushed some makeup over my face.

I looked in the mirror and smiled. Today was the day for me to get my man. I was going to comfort him with my pussy and get my third child in the process. I was going to be kind, sweet, thoughtful, and gentle, all what that bitch no longer was. Now that she was gone, he would finally see me and what he wants. Law had always loved me but he was just blinded by her pretty ass, but now she was a crispy pussy bitch.

What are you laughing at?

I should have felt bad for the bitch but I didn't. She stepped in out of nowhere and took over somebody else's life. I didn't feel bad one single bit. She obviously pissed somebody else off with her perfect black ass and they took her out.

I imagined her screaming out for Law while burning, and that shit made me horny than a motherfucker.

I gathered the kids quickly and left out to drop them off at school before going to fuck my man.

I sang and danced my ass off to the music as I drove towards Law's house. I couldn't wait to feel his dick deep inside of me. My insides tingled as I remembered how good he felt before. Five years I have waited for this and nothing was going to stop me.

When I arrived, I parked my car and walked up to his gates. It was locked with two guards standing outside. I've not seen it locked down like that in years.

"Where do you think you're going?" a tall,

black, and ugly guard said to me in a disgusting tone.

"I'm here to see Law," I said but they didn't move. "Excuse me! Can you move?" I yelled at them.

"You can't come in here. So back up," he barked at me.

"Like hell. Do you know who I am? Open this gate," I yelled.

"Yeah we know exactly who you are Monae. And your ass isn't allowed in here and you know it!" the other guard said and laughed. I was about to snap on their asses when the gate opened and Law's sisters came out followed by three unknown bitches. Law's sisters growled "yuck" at me and continued past me.

"Bitches," I mumbled and when I turned around, I was surrounded by the three ladies.

"Can I help you?" I asked but they just stepped closer to me.

"Yeah, we heard that you like to try jump people," one short fair skinned girl said to me.

I looked over her head at the guards and they just stood there watching.

"I swear to God, y'all motherfuckers better open these motherfucking gates!" I yelled loudly until his neighbors started to come outside to look.

113

"I'm so glad Honey knocked this bitch on her ass. You're nothing but a weak, punk ass bitch. And I should beat your motherfucking ass for even thinking of stepping to my homegirl," the same short lady roared at me. She took one step towards me and then I looked up to see Law standing there.

I smirked when he made them leave. When my girls and I surrounded Honey at the mall, she didn't look scared at all, but I'm not going to lie they had my ass shook.

I was happy to see Law but he didn't seem pleased to see my ass at all.

I lost my mind when he told me that my ass was banned from going to his and Honey's house!!!! That bitch was still alive; you could have told a bitch!

I was hoping she was done for, but instead, that fire did nothing but secure my worst nightmare. Law had moved her into his home, and now there was no way I could get at her with her being there. He made his feelings clear and left me there looking stupid.

My life was officially over. There was no way I could compete with that. He moved her ass in and I know he did it because he wanted her there. Because she wasn't a broke bitch and he had money for days, so between them, they could have easily found her somewhere else to live. This bitch was living my dream. Not only did she live in his house like a queen, but she shared his world, the world that no one ever got the chance to. It was handed to her in a matter of weeks.

I spent the rest of the day in a daze. This had to be a nightmare, this couldn't be real. Law was in love with somebody else. How could that be? She didn't have his kids. I did.

I blamed my parents for this shit. If my daddy had never left, I wouldn't have had such a shitty life to the point that I wanted to fuck around with wealthy niggas just to be looked after. I could have been like Honey, and then Law would have wanted me like he wanted her. They fucked my life up with their selfish asses.

As I collected the kids from school, I couldn't help but hate them. They were supposed to secure my future with Law but they didn't affect or change shit.

In fact, he hated my ass more because they were there. If I hadn't gotten pregnant, Law probably would have started fucking me regularly, but he didn't because I got pregnant.

I couldn't even look at them. I just opened the

door and let them climb in the back of the car.

My anger grew as they sat in the back talking about daddy and Honey. It should have been daddy and mommy, not that life stealing bitch.

"Mommy, are we going to Daddy's now?" Chyna asked.

"No, Chyna."

"But you said you were going to get daddy and we would be a family again. So, I want to go to Daddy's and see Honey as well."

"We are not going to Daddy's and you're not going to see Honey," I yelled at her.

"But, Momma—" she managed to say before I reached back and smacked her.

"Shut the fuck up, Chyna, before I beat your ass again!" I screamed.

She held her face and looked out of the window not saying a word. Mani started hollering and shaking. I gave him one look and he stopped.

Honey had even corrupted my kids; I needed to fuck her up some way or another.

I had a plan before that I put on the back burner, but I guess I had no choice but to go with it.

\*\*\*

## Killa

When I showed up at Honey's apartment, I had a plan of burning it to the ground, which would then force her to come back home, but someone beat me to it. I didn't want her harmed. I knew she wasn't there because I had Dog watching her for me and she was with Law.

It was a fool proof plan. I mean surely she wouldn't move in with Law after only knowing him for a month, but I couldn't have been any more wrong. She didn't even hesitate or attempt to find a hotel. She just gladly moved in with him.

It was the worst thing that could have happened, and if I knew who did it, I would have killed them myself. All they did was fuck my life up more.

I was tapped out. I didn't know what else to do to get Honey back. I had no choice but to wait on Blacka. But as the days went on, I lost more and more confidence that something was going to happen as he looked like he was losing his damn mind.

There was no way I could get at Honey living in Law's house. He had increased security around the both of them, which I'm not surprised about. Somebody tried to kill her. I would do the same thing too. But who could have done that and why?

I sat home alone and annoyed. It wasn't what I expected to happen. Honey should have come back to me. How could she move in with Law so quickly? I remembered we were together for a year before she would move in with me. Could she really love him more than she loved me? Things I had to work years for, he's gotten in a matter of weeks.

My doorbell rang and I was expecting it to be Blacka, but I was surprised when it was a female. She was a pretty redbone with a nice figure. The white dress she had on, fitted her body nicely and enhanced her titties. I unlocked my door and pulled it open.

"Excuse me, ma, do I know you?" I asked and she pushed her way into my house.

"No, but your bitch is fucking my baby daddy," she fumed.

"Now I'm sure you want your girl back, right?" she said and I nodded. "Good because we need to break them up. So, it's either you're going to help me do it or I will kill the bitch. Law is my nigga and not anyone else's. She's lived my life long enough. Now I have a plan."

I looked her up and down for a minute. She wasn't bad looking at all, not Honey but better than the thots I had been fucking with; and since I killed Trixie, I didn't have anyone decent to get pussy from.

"What's in it for me to help your ass? I can get Honey back on my own if I wanted to," I said and smiled. The truth was I was tapped the fuck out on ideas to get her back, but ma didn't need to know that. I wanted pussy, so she better pay the fuck up.

She must have read my mind because she lifted her dress over her head and threw it on the floor. She unhooked her bra and threw it on the floor too.

I grabbed her and threw her down face first on my couch. I ripped her panties off and stuck my tongue straight into her pussy. I licked and slurped on it before pushing two fingers deep inside. Her pussy was warm and wet as fuck. I pulled my fingers out and sucked on them.

I stood to my feet and unzipped my pants and drove my dick into her pussy. I grabbed her by the waist and drilled her forcibly. I smacked her ass and dug as deep as my dick could go. Ma was a beast because her pussy took it all.

Seconds later I'd busted all of my seeds inside of her. She fell on my couch and looked up at me. I could see why Law was fucking my girl; ma's pussy wasn't all that good, but I wasn't about to let her ass know that. For now, she would serve a purpose for moderate pussy and help to get Honey back.

I wiped my dick clean with a cloth and fixed my

clothes. She picked up her dress and put it back on but her panties were done for.

"I'm listening," I said and she smiled.

# Chapter Nine

*Honey*

A few days had passed since my apartment was burned to the ground. Ky-mani went and viewed it for me because I just couldn't bring myself to do it. I had just stopped crying so I knew seeing it would start things off again.

He told me it was nothing but an empty shell full of ash.

The only thing I was grateful for was that none of my neighbors' property was damaged in it. I would have felt even worse if it had.

Ky-mani and his friends decided to throw a barbecue down at the community center. My girls were busy so I went alone with his friends. I didn't mind though because for the last few days he had been by my side doing everything and anything to cheer me up. It was time I did something that he wanted to do.

I wore a black maxi dress with sandals, and he wore a black v-neck t-shirt and black True Religion jeans and black Air Forces. I loved how he looked good in any style of clothes. He had that sexy swag that I loved so much.

We arrived at the center and I could hear music blasting as we walked around to the front of the building. Ricky was out front smoking and talking to another man. They stopped talking when they saw us.

"What's happening, Cuz?" he said, embracing Ky-mani.

"What's good, Cuz?" Ky-mani dapped him.

"Hey, Miss Honey, how you doing?" Ricky hugged me.

"I'm good thank you, Ricky. How are you doing?" I asked as we made small talk.

The other man stood up and approached me.

"So you are the lady who captured my boy's heart? Welcome to the family, Honey, I'm Cameron, Ricky's big brother," he said giving me a quick hug.

We brought our conversation inside. I was pleased to see Toya and Nevaeh were there. So, after talking a little with the guys, I went over to them.

"Hey, sis, what's happening?" Toya said as she hugged me and pulled me down to sit next to her. "I see Ky-mani dragged your ass out," she laughed.

"Yeah, he wanted to meet up with his friends, so I thought I would come along," I smiled.

"Next time stay home," Nevaeh laughed. "All they gone do is play damn dice," she moaned and I laughed.

"I don't mind. If he's happy that's all good to me. He's been in the house with me for days. I just wanted him to get out and chill for a minute," I said and they both nodded.

I looked over and Ky-mani was smiling at me as he sat surrounded by his friends. I knew they were talking about me. I could tell by the way he was smiling so hard at me. I waved at him and smiled back.

I loved when he was happy and not stressing. I didn't want him worrying about me all the time. Just like he knew I needed my friends to cheer me up, I knew he needed to be around his people to occupy his mind with something else.

The DJ was playing some nice beats, so the girls and I got up to dance. Ky- mani kept his eyes on me but I didn't mind. I guess he was just making sure I was enjoying myself and I actually was. I looked over at him and then I caught his uncle's eyes. He was staring at me but without any expression. He was neither happy nor sad to see me, but he just stared at me. After a few more seconds, he finally turned his head and went back to his dice game.

I thought he was just checking me out for his nephew and so I dismissed it. I guess in his line of work; trust was something that didn't come easy. He was never rude to me so I didn't take it personally. They must have been through it all as a family, so him being cautious made sense. Sooner or later, he will realize that I loved Ky-mani and meant him no harm.

I laughed as KY got up to dance to some Rick Ross that was pumping. This fool had two damn left feet and not an ounce of rhythm but he was going hard.

The girls and I couldn't contain our laughter and neither could the boys.

"He can't dance for shit but you gotta love him," Toya yelled over the music and we continued to laugh.

Ky-mani kept smiling at me with his beautiful, handsome self. His eyes glistened from the other side of the room which made my heart melt.

"Look at y'all flirting and smiling at each other like a couple of kids," Momma Doreen said startling me.

"I have never ever seen my son like that Honey, and I love it, and I love you," she said, hugging and kissing me on my cheeks.

"I love your son, Momma Doreen; he makes me feel alive and so happy," I told her and she smiled.

"I'm glad because I know he feels the same way. It's still early days for you two, but I pray every day that y'all will make it; get married, and experience a wonderful life like I did with Malik. He was my best friend and my whole

124

world," she said, tearing up.

"What you two have is special and so real. Hold on to it, Honey, no matter what," she said and kissed me one last time before walking away.

I looked over at Ky-mani and he was still staring at me. He made me blush the way he watched me. It was like he was seeing me again for the first time.

The DJ changed the music to slow jams and Ky-mani stood to his feet. He excused himself and walked towards me.

"Hey, beautiful," he smiled and stroked my face.

He pulled me into him and we started to dance slowly and intimately to the angelic voice of John Legend.

"You know we gonna dance like this at our wedding," he said and I laughed.

"Oh we getting married, are we?" I asked and he nodded.

His family started whooping and cheering as we danced away. I covered my face laughing and Ky-mani waved his hand in the air.

This was such a perfect moment considering what happened only a few days ago. I was enjoying being with Ky-mani and his family was so nice to me. I even loved living with him. It felt so good sleeping next to him with his strong arms wrapped tightly around me. He never slept unless

I was on him or his arms were around me.

We had the best time together, forever laughing and talking. Maybe what I felt going wrong before was my apartment, because things were good, even better than good. And although it was devastating losing all that I worked for, it brought me and Ky-mani even closer together.

I loved him and I loved the kids so much. I couldn't be happier even if I tried.

We socialized for a few more hours with everybody before we left out hand in hand.

We strolled leisurely in the moonlight, holding hands and smiling at each other. I was in awe and beyond happy. Nothing could go wrong…

That was until I turned around. "Ky-mani!!!!"

***

### Law

### Earlier

I smiled as Honey sat talking to my sisters. The way she made them laugh, made me smile. Her presence was so intoxicating. She looked at me and smiled her big sexy smile that I loved so much.

"What's up my niggas?" I heard and I looked up to see Leeroy James, a friend from school. He moved away from Chicago after our school closed down, but we always remained in contact. He recently hit me up because he was looking to buy a property from me and move back into town.

"Yo, Leeroy, what's happening?" I said and dapped him up.

"Shit just chilling. Cameron hit me up and let me know y'all were here so I thought I would pass through. How's the king doing?" he chuckled and I laughed.

"All good in my hood, my nigga," I said.

"How are you finding it being back home?" Camasked him.

"Good, like I never left. I even saw this caramel goddess; mama was motherfucking bad, my niggas," he said smiling.

"Nigga been back a few days and already

127

scoping out females. So, you get her?" Ricky asked.

"Nah, mama shut my ass down!" he said and we all started laughing at him.

"Nigga, you lying," I said and he shook his head.

"For real, my nigga. You know me and how I do. I was spitting all the lyrics at her, ma I got money like that, I'm cute like that, all of that shit. Ma wasn't biting anything. She looked at my ass and was like 'my nigga takes care of all my wants and needs. Can't you see me sitting here in an Armani dress and Giuseppes on my feet,'" he said, mimicking a female's voice and we were dying laughing at him.

"She even shut my ass down when I was like, 'yeah but I'm fine'. She was like, 'you ain't seen, my nigga! Ain't no one walking around who look like him. He's life!'" he continued and I couldn't help but laugh my ass off.

The others started making fun of him.

"I swear I walked in feeling a thousand feet tall but I left feeling one-foot- tall, the way she cut me down to size. I ain't gonna lie though, I was jealous of her nigga. Y'all hardly hear me talk about females and how they look. But when I say momma was fine,

fine ain't even the word. She was fucking beautiful,"
he said I shook my head because I knew he was all in
his feelings about her.

I looked up at Honey and smiled.

"Nigga who the fuck you keep smiling at?" he
asked me and I laughed.

"Oh, this nigga right here has been playing
wave tag with his woman, giving her googly eyes and
shit. His ass in love," Drake said making everyone
laugh. I stuck my middle finger up at him.

"Oh shit, who's the unfortunate woman?"
Leeroy asked and I laughed.

Before I could respond, he looked up and
pointed at Honey.

"Oh shit, y'all know her?" he said.

"That's my girl," I said, looking at him.

"That's your girl?" Leeroy asked and I
nodded.

"Damn, I didn't know that," he said and I
looked at him like 'What?!'

"You know my girl or something?" I asked
with my heart racing. I thought I had a good
relationship with Honey. We told each other
everything about our past. So, I was sure she told

129

me that Jerome was her only boyfriend of any kind...

"Not how you think, my nigga, but that's the girl I was spitting to at the accounting firm and she shut my ass down!" he said and everybody fell out laughing.

"Yo, Law, your girl be knocking bitches out with one punch and making niggas cry. She the boss for real, my nigga. I ain't even fucking with her no more before she murks my ass," Drake said and we all laughed.

"She told me about that. Said some client hit on her but she shut it down. That was you, my nigga?" I laughed and he nodded laughing.

"For real, dog, no bullshit, she shut me all the way down. She loves you in a way I wish I could get. Her eyes were all sparkling and shit when she spoke about you. For real, you got it good, my friend," he said, shaking my hand.

I couldn't help but look back at her. She was my world and I was glad to know I was all that to her too. I knew Leeroy from back in the day; he could charm the panties off any woman. He wasn't lying when he said his pockets flowed deep. He was a well-known music producer and people  paid  top dollar just to sit with him. I ain't gay or anything, but he wasn't an ugly nigga by far.

There wasn't a woman I knew he laid eyes on and didn't get. He had it like that. I remembered when he fucked a woman in the changing rooms as her husband waited for her to try on some clothes she wanted to buy. One look  from Leeroy and her husband was a distant memory.

So, I knew he wasn't lying when he said he tried every trick in the book to holler at   Honey, but she was all mine. I had to admit, hearing her say the things she did about me, made my head swell something big…and I wasn't talking about the one on my shoulders!

When the DJ switched up the music, I knew that was my cue to dance with my baby. Fuck who was in the room. Those niggas couldn't say shit because when their asses were sprung on a female, they weren't any different.

The future flashed through my mind as we danced and it looked good from my side. Honey as my wife and having my babies.

131

I dapped it up with my boys and headed off home with my queen. After talking to Leeroy and hearing what Honey said about me, it had me on another level of love for her. As we walked hand in hand back to my car, I was so into Honey that I was caught snoozing, and before I realized, it was too late.

"Ky-mani!!!" Honey screamed out and I turned to see a hooded nigga swinging a motherfucking steel bat at me but Honey blocked him. She swung her purse, hitting him in the face. I went to grab him but I was pulled back and hit by two other niggas.

They were trying to pin me to the ground, but I was fighting trying to get to Honey. She was tussling with the nigga and he was handling her ass but she didn't stop. He swung and hit her so hard, she flew across the ground.

He grabbed the bat again but she kicked him in his balls causing him to drop it. I did everything I could to get up to her, but these two niggas wouldn't let up. Fear for Honey and rage filled me and I blacked out.

I grabbed one of the niggas and snapped his neck. His body dropped to the ground. But then out of nowhere, three more niggas rushed me.

They were kicking and punching me all over and trying to get me down but I stood my ground. I tried to look up for Honey but my view was being blocked.

I backed up to a wall and let loose on them motherfuckers. My daddy taught me how to box when I was young and all that he taught me came rushing back. I swung and hit one nigga so hard that his nose split open and blood started leaking.

I felt relief when I heard my niggas running towards me. Cameron took one out with a four-hit combo, and Ricky pistol-whipped another. I handled the last one. I instantly turned to look for Honey but Ricky stopped me and started laughing.

Honey had taken the bat and was beating the fuck out of the nigga who was now unconscious. Her eyes were closed as she continued to rain blow after blow onto his body.

"Baby, it's ok. It's ok," I grabbed around her waist and took the bat away.

She turned into my chest and cried bitterly. I

could feel her body shaking.

Ricky ran off to get his truck. KY, Drake, and Cameron picked up the bodies and dumped them into the back of the truck.

Honey was still hanging on to me crying her eyes out.

"Y'all take these motherfuckers to the warehouse but don't do shit until I get there ok? I'm gonna take Honey home," I said and they nodded before climbing into their cars.

I picked up Honey and carried her to my car. I strapped her in and raced to my momma's house. I didn't know who those niggas were so I damn sure wasn't about to leave Honey alone.

I looked down at my hands and they were all blooded. I turned Honey's face so I could inspect it. She had a bruised lip and a cut on top of her eye. That shit just made me even angrier; I couldn't wait to get back to the warehouse. How dare these niggas jump me and my girl!

When I got to my momma's, she was sitting in the living room.

"Oh my God, what the hell happened?" she screeched as she saw my face and Honey's.

"Ky-mani, what happened? I just left y'all at the barbecue," she said.

"Momma, let me take Honey upstairs and I'll be right back ok?" I said and she nodded and stepped aside.

I carried Honey to my room and brought her into the bathroom. I cut the shower on, removed her clothes, and washed her down. When I dried her off, I inspected her body from head to toe. She had a bruise on the right side of her body, where she fell when he hit her. I kissed it and she rubbed the top of my head. I laid her in bed after putting one of my t-shirts on her.

"Ma, I'm sorry but I have to go ok? But I will be back as soon as possible. Ok?" I said stroking her face.

"I love you, Honey," I kissed her.

"I love you too, Ky-mani."

I walked out of the room; turning off the light.

When I reached the bottom of the stairs my mom was pacing the floor.

"Ky-mani, what the hell happened? You

were both fine less than an hour ago," she said, hugging me.

"Ma, I was walking to my car with Honey and then some niggas jumped on us. One of them had her Ma and I couldn't fucking get to her," I yelled with my chest heaving.

"He fucking hit her; he hit my baby, Ma," I was so angry I needed to break something or hurt someone.

My uncle came out of the room he was in with my aunt Ruth. "Nephew, Ricky called me. What the fuck happened?" he said.

"Unc, some niggas tried to get my ass when I was with Honey. The boys have them down at the place. I need to roll out," I said.

I promised my mom I would be back and jumped in my car, heading to the warehouse. My uncle wanted to come but I needed him watching the women just in case somebody tried to go for them.

When I pulled up at the warehouse, I hoped my niggas listened and didn't do shit; especially to the one who had Honey. His ass was mine.

Inside, I found my niggas sitting and puffing

on blunts. How could a good evening go so wrong and so quick?

"Did these motherfuckers say anything?" I asked them.

"Nope, we were waiting for you. We didn't ask them shit yet. Cam tied their mouths up," Ricky said.

"Where's the one who had Honey?" I asked and they pointed to the one in the middle.

I rolled my sleeves up as I walked towards him. I grabbed my black leather gloves from the side and put them on. I grabbed a machete and dragged it across the floor. When I was in front of him, I pulled him up by his hair so he could look me in the eyes when I ended his life. He winced in pain when I dug the blade into his hand.

"What happened to his jaw?" I asked with my eyes still glued on this motherfucker.

"I think Honey broke it with the bat," Cameron said.

"Even better," I said with a smile.

I kicked him on his leg, breaking it instantly.

"I am who I am, so I'm used to niggas being at my head. It went with the territory. But you, you went after my wife. MY WIFE! You hit her like she was a fucking dude!!" I yelled, bringing the machete down on his right hand, cutting it off at the wrist.

He moaned out in pain. I then gave him two punches to the face before slicing an ear off. I hit him with a few punches to his ribs cracking a few in the process. I just couldn't get over the way he hit Honey in her face. He had me fucked up. I cut off his left hand and dropped the machete back on the table, picking up an army knife. He was barely moaning after all the blood he lost, but he was still alive...for now.

I dragged a chair loudly against the floor and positioned it in front of him. I sat on the chair and stared at him. I lifted his head again so he could feel my last words.

"You tried to take my heart when you fucked with her. So, allow me to return the favor," I said and plunged the knife into his chest. I carved his heart right out of his chest and held it in my hand.

"Damn, nigga! That's some Freddie Kruger kind of shit," KY said.

I got up from the chair and dropped the heart in my tank of piranhas. "Cameron grab that AK for me, so I can wrap this shit up and go home to my

138

woman," I said as I washed the blood off my hands.

We were all shocked when we heard the gun go off, as Cameron aired out the rest of the niggas.

"Cam, you're supposed to kill them AFTER you get information from them," Ricky said, shaking his head.

"How the fuck am I supposed to know that? Y'all motherfuckers gave me the gun. I'm not from the streets; I know pussy! Pussy! Y'all got me out here beating on people, running around, abducting people and shit, I'm fucking tired! I'm going home to get some pussy!" he whined, walking towards the door.

We all laughed at him and shook our heads.

I called the clean-up crew and headed home to my woman.

## Chapter Ten

*Law*

When I made it back to my momma's, I was glad that nobody was up waiting for me. I just wanted to be near Honey and not spend all night talking about what happened.

I quietly crept into my room so I wouldn't wake Honey. She was lying on her side curled in a ball. I continued to walk past her and went into the bathroom. I didn't want to go near her dirty and with blood on me. Thank God I was wearing black today. I pulled everything off and dropped them in the incinerator in the back room. I grabbed a washcloth and jumped in the shower.

I scrubbed my skin making sure nothing was left behind before I got in bed with Honey.

She was sitting up in bed when I walked back in. My heart broke as I saw her bruised face. I turned off the light and dropped my towel. I crawled up the bed and dropped my lips onto hers. She wrapped her arms around my neck and deepened the kiss.

I pulled my t-shirt over her head and kissed down her body until I reached her breasts. I kissed and licked on them, making her twist her body in pleasure.

I licked down from her breasts until I reached the top of her panties. I slid my fingers over the rim and gently trailed them down her legs.

I parted her legs and sucked softly on her pussy. She moaned quietly and wrapped her hand around my dreads. I kissed her for a few more seconds before positioning my dick at her opening and sliding in.

I had to pause for a minute before I busted. Her pussy gripped me tighter than a new born baby's grip.

She quietly cried out as her body accommodated my size.

Finally, I was feeling my baby and she felt motherfucking good.

I looked down at her and searched her eyes. Despite what happened earlier, this moment felt so right.

She smiled up at me and I dropped my lips onto hers. I pushed in and out of her slowly with long deep strokes. She clawed at my back and wrapped her legs tightly around me. I pushed deeper and sighed out. Honey had my head in the clouds. I continued thrusting as she moaned out my name.

I rolled over and she climbed on top. She dropped that pussy on me and I almost cried out for my momma. She bounced and twerked on my dick. Her pussy was so warm and wet just the way I liked it.

Her breasts bounced up and down making a fucking good sight. I grabbed them, pushed them together, and licked across both nipples.

"Damn, baby," I whispered.

I flipped her over onto her knees and licked up and down her juicy, sweet pussy before inserting my dick again. She popped her pussy on me and backed her ass up on me making it clap with each thrust. My baby was bad and my ass was hooked. Her pussy was to die for and kill for. I wasn't ever letting her ass go. If she didn't know, you better know that I just sealed us together once and for all.

I pushed her shoulders down onto the bed, leaving her booty in the air. I grabbed her waist and thrust rapidly. She threw her pussy back at me, matching my pace.

"Oh shit," she cried and bit into the pillow. She used it to muffle her cries as she came on my dick. I looked down as I pulled out slowly and my dick glistened in the dark from all her juices. I pushed back deeply inside to the very end of my dick.

I tapped my foot on the bed as I shook and trembled, releasing my seeds. I rotated my hips into her for a few more seconds, salvaging the wonderful feeling, before I dropped back on the bed. I was out of breath and breathing heavy with a huge smile on my face. That was worth the wait!

She kissed me before climbing off the bed and grabbing damp washcloths to clean us off. When she was done, she climbed onto my chest and hugged me.

"I was so scared tonight Ky-mani," she hugged me tightly. "When I turned and saw the bat, I panicked. I thought that they were going to take you from me and the kids. But when I got the bat, all I kept thinking was what if he did? What if I never saw the bat? He would have killed you and taken you from us. I blacked out as I hit him," she said and I could feel her tears wetting my chest.

"Ma I'm sorry you were scared. I'm sorry you had to experience that and that I couldn't get to you," I said, rubbing her back and kissing her head.

"I love you, Ky-mani, and I don't want you to ever leave me. I wanted to kill him," she said, looking up at me. I stroked her beautiful face and wiped her tears away.

"You don't have to worry about that. I'm not going anywhere," I said and she smiled.

"Are they gone?" she asked and I knew what she meant. I didn't want her to know and fear me again but I didn't want to lie to her.

"Yes," I admitted.

"Good! I'm glad," she said and laid her head back down on me.

"I don't want you to be scared of me, Honey. As long as I live, I would never hurt you," I said and she stroked my face.

"I know, Ky-mani, and I'm not afraid. They had to go so they couldn't try to hurt us again. The kids and I need you. Your momma needs you, your sisters, your whole family; we need you. And nobody who wants to take you away from us can stick around," she said and I kissed her.

I rolled her over and crawled in my pussy over and over again until we both fell asleep exhausted.

In the morning, I kissed Honey's naked back and climbed out of bed. My baby looked good sleeping naked but she felt even better. I went into the bathroom and brushed my teeth. I was mad when I saw the bruising on my face. Since Cameron killed them before I could talk to them, I needed to hit the streets to find out who they were. I jumped in the shower and washed off. Halfway through, I felt Honey's soft hands on me.

Instantly, my dick was hard. I grabbed her and kissed her. I pushed her up against the wall, picked her up and slid her down on my dick.

"Ahh, Ky-mani," she cried and dropped her head on my shoulder. I pinned her back against the wall and went in for the kill.

"Shit, Honey, shit!" I hissed as her pussy muscles massaged my dick with her tight embrace.

I circled my dick to the left and then the right as I dug deep inside and she went ballistic. She held on to my neck and leaned back as she bounced herself on my dick. I grabbed her breast with one hand and gripped her booty with the other.

She rotated her hips and circled on my dick, sending my eyes into the back of my head.

"Ahh!" we both moaned as we came together. I dropped my hand on the wall to hold myself up.

She went to stand but her legs were like jelly.

"Damn, I messed you up, ma?" I laughed and she

smacked me. We washed each other off, got dressed, and raced downstairs.

My momma jumped up and hugged us as we walked into the living room.

She then examined Honey's face and looked up at me.

"I know, ma. But he looked worse in the end," I said and she nodded. She never liked when I killed people but she understood that it was necessary.

"I'm ok, Momma Doreen," Honey smiled and my momma kissed her cheeks.

My unc got up and hugged me. Then he patted Honey on the shoulder and we all laughed. I guess he was warming up to her.

My sisters both embraced Honey. Things could have been so much worse last night. Who knows what those niggas would have done or what that nigga planned on doing to Honey. I knew at one point I saw him grabbing on her body trying to feel on her. I knew in my heart if she hadn't fought back, he was going to rape her and maybe have me watch.

I'm not jumping to conclusions, but they were trying to knock me out and pin me down, not kill me. If they wanted me dead, they would have brought guns not a bat. That nigga grabbed Honey with one hand and swung at my head with the other; that's how she managed to block him. Why did he grab her first unless he had plans for her?

I looked at Honey and knots battered my stomach. If he had laid hands on her in the way I knew he wanted to, I would have died a thousand deaths.

But as I sat there and watched her, I knew things turned out the way it did because she helped me. Most females would run or scream but Honey fought for me more than herself. She did everything in her power to keep that nigga away from me; even when he hit her, sending her flying, she got back up.

I didn't care that my family was there, I was there because of Honey. I grabbed her and pulled her down onto my lap. I wrapped my hands around her waist and buried my head into her chest. She hugged me tightly and rested her head on mine.

My family just stood there holding hands around us. They knew what I knew; Honey saved a nigga's life, that's for sure.

"I love you so fucking much, Honey," I said teary eyed.

"I love you more, Ky-mani," she whispered and I felt her tears drop on my head.

I looked up into her beautiful eyes and wiped her tears away. "It's you and me baby," I smiled, stroking her face.

"You better believe it, baby," she smiled and we kissed.

"Will y'all motherfuckers just please get married and

put us out of our misery," Ricky said as he and the boys walked in.

"Only if your ass is a bridesmaid," Honey said and we all fell out laughing our asses off.

"That's my queen," I said, kissing her again.

She climbed off of my lap and pulled me up. My momma made breakfast, so we all sat down to eat as a family.

Before long, my niggas and I needed to hit the streets.

"Ma, I need to hit these streets, and see if anyone knows anything. You stay here with my family but I will be back as soon as I can. I love you, alright?" I said, holding her chin and looking into her hazel eyes.

"I love you too. Please be safe Ky-mani and come back to me."

"Always," I said and kissed her.

I left my unc in charge and rode out with my boys.

"First my girl's house is burned down and now some niggas tried to grab my ass last night. I never told y'all, but that nigga was grabbing on Honey like he wanted to rape her or some shit. And those other niggas were trying to get me down on the ground; they weren't trying to kill me. What the fuck did they want?" I roared and punched my steering wheel.

"My bad, cuz, I shouldn't have taken them out. I'm sorry," Camsaid.

"Nah, G, you're good, you didn't know," I said because he didn't. He wasn't from the streets, Papa De taught me that shit; I didn't just know it. So, I couldn't expect Cam to.

I drove around town to make my presence known. It had been a minute since my ass was on the blocks like that, but it needed to be done. I stopped every nigga and bitch I saw and questioned them. But we didn't get anything solid. One thing I knew for sure, I had never seen those niggas before. They were some out of town cats; which would mean, another nigga was at my head for my crown.

I stopped by all of my trap houses and told everyone to be on alert and to beef up security. I then headed off to my office at the club. I called a few of my business associates to see if they heard anything while Cam, Drake, and KY wandered the streets.

"Cuz, you really think another cat from outta town is on you?" Ricky asked me.

"Bro, I ain't never seen them niggas before. And like I said, they weren't trying to kill me, their asses wanted something," I said and he nodded.

Usually, someone would have claimed to be behind it by now but the streets were quiet and whoever those niggas worked for was even quieter.

"What's good, boss?" KY said as he bopped into my office followed by Drake and Cam.

"Y'all heard anything?" I asked.

"I made some calls home. Apparently, they were some young niggas from Detroit. They wanted to rob you, cuz. They planned to kidnap you and Honey, and fuck her until you gave them all the money you had," Cam said and I looked at him.

"What, now?" I asked with my brows narrowed tight.

"Yeah, that's the word in Atlanta. How much of that is true, I do not know. But explains why no one here knows shit. Those niggas rode in last night from outta town," he said.

I heard him but I didn't hear him. It added up from what I said about one grabbing on Honey and the fact they had no guns. I knew he was right when he said they wanted something from me. But I wasn't under any impression that it started and ended with them! Someone was behind that shit; someone else and someone big. And since their ass didn't get what they wanted, I knew their ass was coming back…but harder.

I didn't share my thoughts; I just kept it to myself. Ricky

150

looked at me and I knew he was reading my thoughts. We were connected like that. He nodded his head at me and I did the same.

*The first thing I need to do is move with Honey*, I thought to myself. There was a house I was eyeing for some time that was a little further than River North, about forty minutes from my momma; a huge gated nine-bedroom mansion with a security tower and electrified gates. I would have to redo the inside how I wanted, but she was a beauty.

First thing in the morning I was making that shit mine and Honey's.

I sent a text to my realtor and told her to line that shit up. I smiled when I thought about me buying a house with a woman for the first time. I knew Honey and the kids would love it. Speaking of kids, I needed to check on them.

I sent Monae a message and told her that I would be getting them in a few days.

I checked in with my uncle and the ladies were in the pool having a good old time. I felt bad leaving him to be the only nigga in the house with four females, but they needed someone around just in case.

The boys chilled for a while, chatting shit up as usual

151

until they all left out, except Ricky.

He didn't say much but his company spoke volumes. He knew I was in my thoughts but he stayed with me just in case I needed him. Ricky was my right- hand man, I had been around him every day for twenty-nine years; we were only six months apart, me being older. And as you probably noticed, our mothers were inseparable. He was like my brother more than my cousin. We knew each other's thoughts and had each other's backs. I could never imagine my life without him.

My buzzer went off and I looked up at Ricky first before turning to look at my monitor.

*What the fuck she wants now?* I thought to myself as I saw Angel outside the door. I hadn't really seen or spoken to Angel since before I met Honey.

I heard she was at my birthday party but I never saw her as I was so busy with Honey.

She had been my side piece for about a year; a pretty, dark-skinned Jamaican girl that I fucked with from time to time. She never gave me any grief and never came out of her lane, unlike Monae's ass. But before I met Honey, I just kind of stopped seeing her; no particular reason, but it just stopped.

152

I think I was more interested in getting a wife than pussy and although she was aight and all, she wasn't what I wanted for a wife. She seemed cool the last time I did see her and understood when I said I was not about that life anymore.

Other than me calling her for pussy back in the day, she had never just shown up where I was at. So seeing her at my door, had my mind all over the place.

"She better not be on no bullshit. I don't have time for this," I said to Ricky as I buzzed her in.

I needed to be figuring shit out; I didn't have time to be talking to no damn female about anything. If it wasn't going to benefit me and my situation, then I didn't want to know.

She came up into my office and looked shocked to see Ricky. "Hey, Law. I was hoping I could talk to you…in private," she said.

"Nah, ma, Ricky is cool. Whatever you want to talk about you can say it in front of him," I said and she bucked her eyes at me.

"Unless your ass came in here looking dick. And in that case, you out of luck because there's only one pussy that's tasting this dick and that's my woman," I said and she rolled her eyes at me and sucked her teeth.

153

Ricky started laughing and flamed up a blunt.

"Yeah I saw you with your bitch," she snapped and I looked up at her.

"Watch your motherfucking mouth, bitch!" I growled at her.

"You quick enough to fuck me but as soon as lil' miss pretty bitch arrives; it's fuck me, nigga!" she pointed at me.

"Bitch, my ass was done with you long before I met Honey. I've known her two months. I ain't fucked yo ass in almost four. The fuck you mean!" I stood to my feet yelling at her.

Ricky wasn't shit because his ass sat there with a damn smirk on his face looking from me to her like his ass was watching fucking tennis or something.

"Yeah whatever because we both know if she wasn't around, your ass would still be knee deep in this pussy," she crossed her arms and I chuckled.

"Ma, trust and believe your pussy wasn't all that," I said and Ricky burst out laughing until his ass started coughing and choking.

"Yeah, well we will see about that when your bitch leaves your ass! Congratulations, motherfucker, you're gonna be a daddy!" she said, opening her coat to reveal a small, round baby bump.

"Fuck me!"

# Chapter Eleven

***Honey***

My face had finally started to heal after that nigga hit me. He hit me so hard that my ears started to ring, but I knew I had no choice but to try and fight back. I had to keep him from Ky-mani because God knows what would have happened if he got to him.

All I remembered was looking behind me and seeing this hooded figure. At first, I thought it was one of Ky-mani's friends until I saw the bat.

Next thing I knew, the nigga grabbed me and swung at Ky-mani. I automatically grabbed the bat to stop him. I don't even remember getting a hold of the bat or hitting him with it, but when Ky-mani grabbed me around my waist and took the bat from my hands, I broke down.

Nothing but the fear for Ky-mani and pure adrenaline kept me going. But when Ky-mani brought me to his momma's house, I felt the pain and soreness in my body. I bruised the whole right side of my body when I hit the ground.

It was truly a frightening moment but one that

156

strengthened the bond between me and Ky-mani. It elevated the love that we felt for each other and even presented the perfect moment for us to finally make love. There didn't seem like a better moment to seal our love for each other after experiencing such a traumatic event together.

I understood when he said he needed to hit the streets to see if he could find out who was behind it. I know I should have been scared to know he killed those men, but at the same time, I knew it needed to be done. Because I knew if

the tables were turned and they did what they planned to do, those niggas would have killed us without so much of a thought.

And if I was honest, I slept a little better at night knowing that they were no longer around to try and hurt us again.

His family had been great to me since I had arrived. If anything, it made us have a closer bond too. Even his uncle was warming up to me.

I tried my best to wait up for Ky-mani but my body was still sore and tired from tussling with that nigga and the loving Ky-mani put on my body. His dick game was unlike anything else. He made my body do things I didn't even know she could do. His dick was so big, I had to get my body used to him; but once I passed the first initial pain, nothing but

157

pleasure flooded me after that. It was the best I've ever had and well worth the wait. But I knew one thing for sure; we would be at it like rabbits after that point!

I expected him to wake me when he came back, or well, a part of me hoped that he would but as I woke up to find it was morning, I was surprised that I was all alone.

Since I had known Ky-mani and stayed with him, I had never woken up alone. I rolled out of bed and headed to the bathroom to brush my teeth and have a shower. My heart leaped into my throat when I walked back into the room and he was sitting on the bed. He still had on his clothes from yesterday, so I guessed that he hadn't been to sleep yet. He looked weary and tired like he had been up all night stressing about something.

"Good morning, babe. Did you just get back?" I said and he huffed at me.

"No, Honey, I been here. I was just in the living room. I couldn't sleep," he said, rubbing his temples with his eyes closed.

Wow was he annoyed that I asked him a question? I wanted to say more but I just left it alone. His mind was full and I could understand that. He must have been racking his brain roaming the streets trying to find out who those men were. I couldn't fault him for being a little edgy.

"Ok, Ky-mani," I smiled and gave him a kiss. When my lips touched his, the kiss felt strained and not how he usually did. I wasn't sure what to say so I shook it off. Something was off but I guess he would tell me when he wanted to.

"I got a meeting in a bit. I'm buying a new house," he said without much of a tone in his voice. I had been so busy enjoying his company that I hadn't started looking for my own apartment yet. But now he was planning on moving, I needed to get myself in order and quick.

"You're free to come along or you can stay here if you like," he said, not sounding too bothered either way.

I tried to brush off his whole demeanor from the outset, but the more I tried, the more he was straight upsetting my ass. I thought that it would be best if he just went alone, so I declined the half bullshit offer. He stood up and started to take off his clothes but I headed for the door and he grabbed me back.

"I'm sorry, baby. I'm sorry. It's just that I'm stressing about some things and I'm taking it out on you," he said, resting his head on top of mine with his eyes closed.

That was the first time he ever made me feel like I was bugging him and it was a feeling that I did not like at all. I knew he was sorry but at the same time, I didn't want to be his mental punching bag. So, for today I was going to stay out of his way.

"It's ok, Ky-mani. I understand you're going through something and I don't want to add to it at all. I will stay here today so I'm not in the way. It's ok, I understand," I said and he sighed.

"Honey, I don't want you to ever feel like you're in the way because you never could be. I'm sorry for my behavior. Please come with me," he pleaded and I kissed his lips softly.

"It's ok, Ky-mani. I want to stay," I said and pulled away from him and left the room.

I knew he was sorry but whatever was troubling him was still there, so sooner or later, the attitude was going to resurface. And I just didn't want to spoil anything any more than it was with us arguing.

Plus, I needed to find myself somewhere to live. I didn't want him to feel like he had to move me in with him again.

I sat on the couch and grabbed my iPad from my tote and started browsing for apartments.

"Morning, sis; what's up?" I looked up to see Nevaeh

smiling at me.

"Hey, Nev; morning girl. I'm good. You aight?" I asked, closing my iPad as she slumped on the couch next to me. She rested her head on my shoulder and I held her hand.

"I couldn't sleep for shit. I just kept thinking about the other night and what if they got you guys," she said sadly. "I know we just been knowing you for a few months Honey, but I really do love you. And it scares me when I think about what could have happened," she said and I squeezed her hand.

"I know, sis. I was so damn scared but I was more scared of losing your brother," I said and she nodded her head.

"You really do love him, don't you?" she asked and I sighed.

"More than life," I said and she squeezed my hand.

"And he loves you more than life too," we heard a voice behind us and turned to see Ky-mani standing there looking at us.

Nevaeh kissed my cheek and got up and approached her brother. She gave him a hug and a kiss, then disappeared into the kitchen.

Ky-mani stood there silently looking at the floor with his hands in his pockets.

161

"Honey, I gotta tell you something," he said lowly as his family burst into the living room laughing and talking loudly.

"Good morning, y'all," his momma chimed.

I said good morning and then turned my attention back to Ky-mani. He remained in the same spot, fidgeting and looking down at the ground, before shaking his head at me and following his mom outside.

I didn't see Toya standing there and she looked at me and shrugged her shoulders at me. I guess she saw that too.

I put my iPad away and went outside with the family.

Ky-mani was standing holding a chair out waiting for me. I took a seat mumbling 'thank you' and he pushed it in for me and took the seat next to me.

Earlier when I woke up, I thought his mood had to do with those niggas from the other night, but now I'm convinced it isn't. Maybe it's because of me and if that's the case, I was right to be afraid to fuck him. I just knew in my heart shit would change as soon as I did; I just didn't think that it would that quick.

I literally gave myself to him multiple times that same night and the morning after and I thought all was good. I enjoyed it and I thought he did too from the way he moaned

162

my name; but how wrong was I?

Maybe he was expecting more because he waited so long, I don't know. Sorry to disappoint! I felt so ashamed and down. I didn't even want to sit next to him but I didn't want to cause a scene in front of his family. So, until he returned from his business meeting, purchasing his house or whatever, I will just keep my ass cool until he can take me back to his. And soon as morning broke, I was hauling my ass out of his house. Embarrassed was an understatement!

He tried to make small talk with me during eating but I wasn't biting. I just shook my head, nodded, or shrugged my shoulders to respond to him. I hardly said anything to his family either. They never did anything wrong to me but I just didn't feel like talking. Even his uncle was talking directly to me and smiling; just my luck for him to do it on the day Ky-mani showed his ass.

When we all finished eating, I jumped up and helped Momma Doreen with the plates so I could get away from his ass.

"You ok, baby?" his momma asked as I followed her into the kitchen.

"Yeah, Momma I'm good. I'm just thinking about my family. I miss them," I said. I wasn't lying because I truly was thinking about them and missing them, but the main reason for my mood was because of her son, but she didn't need to know that.

I helped wash up the plates and put away equipment and ingredients that were used. I dried my hands with the dishcloth after washing them and turned to head for my iPad to continue with my search for apartments.

Ky-mani walked into the kitchen as I was about to walk out. He still had the same sad look on his face but I didn't care.

I turned to step right past him but he stepped in my way. "Honey," he said.

"Let me pass, Ky-mani," I said and he shook his head.

Before I could push past him, he grabbed me and picked me up, hugging me from behind.

"Y'all ok?" his momma asked when she saw him do that.

"We good momma," he said as he pulled me into the back room with him. I didn't even fight or say anything because it wouldn't have made a difference. It was nothing for Ky-mani to pick me up so I knew his ass wasn't going to put me down.

He pushed the door to the laundry room with his foot and put me down inside and closed the door.

I folded my hands across my chest and shook my head. He went to talk but I put my hand up to stop him.

"I'm sorry, Ky-mani. I'm sorry that me giving myself to you wasn't what you expected. I'm sorry it wasn't good for you. I'm sorry that you wished it never happened," I said and he rubbed his hand down his neatly cut goatee.

"Is that what you think, Honey?" he said and approached me.

He went to touch my face but I slapped his hand away. He grabbed both my hands in one of his big, strong hands and stroked my face with the other.

"Oh, Honey, is that what you thought? Ma, being with you the other night for the first time was the best feeling ever. It was beyond what I expected and more than worth the wait. I love being with you, making love to you baby. I love you," he said, staring into my eyes.

"So what did I do wrong, Ky-mani?" I whispered emotionally. I couldn't lie and say I wasn't hurt because I was. Things were going so good and then all of a sudden he's acting distant with me, sleeping in the living room instead of the bed with me; practically ignoring me. I would have preferred if he told me what I did, instead of treating me like a leper.

"Baby you didn't do anything wrong and I'm so sorry I

165

made you feel like you did," he pulled me in and kissed me passionately. He pushed his tongue in my mouth and then ran it along my bottom lip before sucking on it followed by the top one.

He kissed me almost like the first time he did at his party but I know something was still holding him back.

"Honey, those niggas from the other night were from Detroit…and they planned…they planned on kidnapping us and…" he sighed and shook his head.

"They were going to rape you continuously until I gave them what they wanted," he finally said and my whole body shook.

"You're my heart, my soul, my world Honey. You're life to me, Honey. Every time I look at you, I wonder what if they did. It makes me so angry; I wish I could murk their asses over and over again. I saw how that nigga was grabbing on you, and I knew what he wanted to do to you," he said and I could see the rage in his eyes.

The only thing I knew to do was hug him tightly.

"It's ok, baby. We're OK, we are safe," I said as he held me tightly.

"Listen Honey they were young cats so I know they were not alone. Whoever sent them is still out there. That's why I'm looking at somewhere else to live, but in the meantime, baby I need you to follow my lead. I'm not trying to control you, but if I say go, I want you to go; and if I say don't, I need you to listen. Can you do that for me, baby?" he asked and I kissed him again.

"Yes, baby, I promise," I said once we broke our kiss.

His phone started ringing and he pulled it out looking at it.

"I gotta go, baby, and see about this house. We will talk later, ok? I love you, Honey, and always will," he said, claiming my lips with his for almost a minute before letting go. He turned and locked the door.

"The realtor can wait five more minutes," he said, picking me up and placing me down on the dryer. He pulled my leggings and panties off and opened my legs. He kissed me while unzipping his pants.

"Sssss," I hissed when I felt his dick enter me.

I wrapped my legs tightly around him and pulled him in deeper between my legs.

"Damn I love you, Honey," he groaned as he thrust deeply in and out of me.

"I. Love. You. Too," I barely managed to say as he dicked my ass down good.

167

I threw my head back, closed my eyes and bit down on my bottom lip.

Nothing but light moans could be heard between us as he continued to fuck me senseless.

"Shit. Shit. Shit," he hissed as he released himself in me.

I was definitely getting my ass back on the Depo shots and soon. The last one was almost up.

He looked down at me breathless and smiled. He grabbed some tissues from a cupboard and gently cleaned me up with them and then himself.

I pulled back on my leggings and panties and he fixed his clothes.

"I have to go, baby, sorry," he kissed me quickly and pulled me out of the back room. Thankfully, his family was all out busy talking in the garden to know what we just did.

He told them all goodbye and giving me one final kiss, he ran out of the door.

I grabbed my iPad and joined his family outside. Nevaeh smiled and winked at me, so I knew she realized what we did. I smiled nervously and buried my face into my iPad.

We all sat outside chatting and laughing. My stomach

was hurting from all the laughing I did when his momma told me stories about the girls and Ky-mani.

"You better watch yourself before he gives your ass bad little versions of him," Momma Doreen said and we all started laughing.

"Do you remember when I was babysitting his little black ass and he wanted to go out but I wouldn't let him. So, he called the cops and said how I wouldn't let him and his sister out. They thought I was kidnapping his ass. Had them motherfuckers kick my door in and shit," Aunt Ruth said making us all laugh.

We were so busy laughing that we didn't notice Ky-mani had come back. I smiled when I saw him and jumped to my feet to kiss him but his face told me better. Was he angry that we were laughing and sharing old time stories?

"Ky-mani, fix your face; we were only playing," his momma stood and kissed his cheek.

He gave a smile but it wasn't his usual smile. He left ok and came back even angrier.

Did the house fall through or something, or did he find something else out on the streets?

I didn't know this Ky-mani and I didn't like him. Maybe this wasn't Ky-mani after all; maybe what I was seeing was, in fact, Law!

He stroked my face and kissed me hard on the lips.

"I'm good, momma," he said and grabbed a seat next to me.

I got up and helped Momma Doreen bring out the food for dinner. Ky-mani watched me intensely as I moved around. He then dropped his eyes to his uncle before looking back up at me.

"Come and sit, ma," he said, pulling me down next to him. He wasn't rough when he did but he wasn't gentle either.

His sisters and mom looked up at him and then looked at me with worried eyes.

What the hell was happening?

"Are you ok?" I asked him and he nodded his head after looking up at his  uncle one more time.

Dinner was a quiet one, nobody spoke a single word. Since I had known them, we never experienced that and by the looks of things, his family didn't know what to do or say either.

When we finished eating, I went to stand to help and he grabbed my hand.

170

"Hold on for a minute, babe," he said and I sat down. I looked over at his momma and she sat back down too. Something was about to kick off but I just didn't know what.

"Toya and Nevaeh, y'all excuse us for a minute," he said. They both looked at their momma and then at him.

"What?" Toya said with an attitude.

"DO WHAT I SAID!" he shouted and slammed his fists down on the table.

We all jumped at his action.

Momma Doreen nodded her head and the girls got up and ran.

"Ky-mani, have you lost your damn mind?" she said, pointing at him.

"Sorry but this ain't even about you, Ma. Yo, Unc," he said and everyone looked up at Ky-mani like he lost his damn mind.

"You gunning for me, young blood?" Marco said, putting his blunt down.

"Well, that depends," Ky-mani said.

"Yeah on what, little nigga?" Marco frowned.

"On if you have a motherfucking eye problem?!" Ky-mani shouted. Marco looked at him and burst out laughing.

"What you on about nephew?" he continued to

171

chuckle.

"Now you're my uncle and all. In every aspect of the word; you're married to my aunt, you're the father to my cousins, the brother in law to my momma, you're family. But, Unc I don't like the way you be eyeing Honey. So, like I said, do you have a motherfucking eye problem," he asked again but this time Marco didn't laugh.

Momma Doreen and Aunt Ruth jumped in and started calling Ky-mani all kinds of crazy but Marco stopped them.

"It's not even like that nephew. I know her people, that's all," he said, picking up his blunt and puffing on it again.

"You know my family?" I asked surprised and he nodded.

"Yeah I know them; your momma, Patrice, your grandma, Naomi, her sister, Julie, your grandpa, Rupert; all of them. How is Rupert doing these days anyway?" he blew smoke from his nose.

"He died a year ago," I said and he looked at me.

"Man, I'm sorry to hear that. I always liked him," he said sincerely.

"So this whole time you knew her people but you didn't say shit and acted like you don't know her or even liked her.

What the fuck is up with that?" Ky-mani demanded.

"I couldn't say anything, nephew. And I couldn't help looking at her. You look so much like your momma, Honey," he said.

"How do you know my family, Marco?" I asked and he just stared at me.

He sat quietly and just faced the blunt before outing it in the ashtray. He exhaled long and hard and rubbed Aunt Ruth on her shoulder. He mouthed 'I love you,' to her and looked over at me.

"I know your family, Honey, because I'm your dad," he said, just like that, like it was nothing. This was some kind of Star Wars, Luke Skywalker, and Darth Vader bullshit. Were there motherfucking cameras somewhere, was Ashton Kutcher gonna jump his scary ass out from a bush or something and punk my ass?

This man who Ky-mani came to know and love as his uncle, was my daddy!?!?

I jumped to my feet and slammed my fists down on the table.

"What the hell did you just say to me?" I yelled in his face.

173

"I'm your dad, Honey," he said, reaching into his wallet and pulling out a photo and handing it to me.

I looked at it and I saw my momma, Marco, and me. He was holding me and kissing my cheek. I looked to be about three or four years old. Tears came to my eyes and I wiped them away frantically. I looked like my momma but I had his eyes. Ky-mani went to hold me but I pushed him off.

"You are not my daddy!" I threw the picture at him.

"For years I wondered who you were and why you never loved me!" I screamed crying.

"I do love you, Honey, I always have. I left to protect you and your momma; I was deep in the streets with Deano when you were little. Some guys came after you and your momma. This is what they did to me," he said, pulling his shirt up and exposing a wound going all the way across his stomach.

"You got a scar on your lower back, don't you?" he said and I nodded.

"I was holding you when I was running. They shot me and you fell. A piece of glass went into your back. We got away but when you were in the hospital I left. Your momma didn't want me to leave but I knew if I didn't, y'all would have been killed because of me. But I've thought about you every single day. When I saw you that day with Ky-mani, I

174

wanted to tell you so badly, baby girl," he said, stepping towards me but I stepped back.

"Ky-mani, take me home," I said.

"Baby let's—" he said but I cut him off.

"TAKE ME HOME!!!" I screamed and ran up into the room I stayed in. I grabbed my duffle bag and started shoving everything I owned in it. I wiped my face as the tears flooded. Ky-mani walked in.

"Honey?" he called me but I ignored him. "Baby, listen to me," he said, grabbing me.

"Ky-mani, please! I can't do this right now. I'm begging you please, take me home. Please!" I pleaded and cried my eyes out.

"Ok, baby, ok," he said, hugging me.

He helped me collect the rest of my stuff that he brought over the night of the barbecue. He grabbed my bag and walked out of the room. As I walked down the stairs, everybody was standing around at the end of the stairs. Marco looked up at me and came to the stairs.

"Baby girl, please let me just explain," he pleaded but I pushed past him and walked out the door.

"Give her time, Unc," I heard Ky-mani say as I walked out the door.

The ride home was a silent one. I can't believe I was right there with my father and didn't even know. I mean, him

175

and I were not the only people with hazel eyes so I wasn't going to think he was my dad just because of them. Like he said, I looked like my mother. Even when he revealed who he was, I still couldn't see any resemblance other than the eyes.

"Is that why you were angry all day because you thought your uncle was watching me?" I broke the silence and said.

"No, that's not why. I admit I was angry thinking it was something else when I saw him looking at you, but that's not why," he said.

"Ok so are you going to tell me, Ky-mani?"

"Baby, I don't think—" he started.

"Ky-mani, tell me please," I cut him off and said.

He kept quiet and focused on the road but I could tell that he was in deep thought.

He huffed and puffed and ran his hand down his face onto his goatee.

"Do you remember when we first got together and I told you that the last time I hooked up with someone was about a month before I met you?" he asked and I swallowed hard.

"Yes, Ky-mani. Did you sleep with her last night or something?" I asked as my stomach turned, filled with anxiety.

"No, baby, no never. Nothing like that. I promise I've never cheated on you," he said, grabbing my hand and kissing the back of it.

"So what is it, Ky-mani? Why did you bring that up then?"

"Because she's three and a half months pregnant," he said and the words slapped me in the face.

I guess when it rains, it motherfucking pours!!!

# Chapter Twelve

*Monae*

"Yes, daddy, give me that dick!" I cried out as Killa dropped that dick on my ass.

"Give me that pussy, ma. Just like that," he moaned as I rode him reversed cowgirl style.

I know what you're thinking. If I'm running down Law, trying to fuck up his relationship with Honey, why am I giving pussy to her ex, Killa? Well for more than one reason. One, he can help me in my plan to destroy their relationship, two, Law will never find out and three, I just love the idea of Honey going back to her ex after I've fucked him.

I really hated that lucky bitch. Killa was a fine nigga with a big dick. Not as fine as Law or as big, but he was a close second.

This bitch had fine ass niggas with money at her disposal. And both of them belonged to her at different points. I've never had a nigga to call my own. Even Pete was my momma's man. And yes, in the end, he thought he was mine and he was cute; like Denzel Washington grown man cute, but he wasn't Killa or Law.

I was so envious of this bitch; I was surprised my skin didn't glow green. When I got Honey's information from her driver's license, I ran a trace on her which is how I found out about Killa.

This bitch had only just left his home that her name was still registered under, and she had already moved in with Law. I couldn't believe it when I pulled up at the address for him and saw this fucking mini mansion. Not as big as what Law had, but for a common low-level nigga, Killa was giving Honey everything that Pete couldn't give me.

And yeah I was taking a risk fucking Killa raw, but I made up my mind that the only kids coming from my pussy would be Law's.

Killa grunted before releasing his seeds all in me.

If I had to keep throwing the pussy at him to get results then so be it.

Law had texted me to say he was going to see the kids in a few days and I had a plan for his ass.

"Ok, can we get down to business now?" I asked Killa after I adjusted my clothes.

"Sure," he said, firing up a blunt.

179

"Ok, so I was thinking that we should get Honey fired," I said and he looked at me.

"She wanna fuck Law, well I'm about to mess up everything surrounding her life," I said laughing.

"And how do you expect us to do that?" he asked and I walked around the room thinking.

"Come on, Killa. You shared a home with Honey for years. Surely she used something of yours that still has her information on it," I said and he looked at me.

"Nothing but email. She used my laptop and sent some emails. When I logged on recently, I saw that it was still open," he said and I smiled.

"Show me," I said and he grabbed it for me.

Sure enough, as soon as I opened it, I saw that it was indeed still opened to her personal email address.

I scrolled through her contacts and then I found her boss' email address.

A wicked smile crept across my face as I sent an interesting email to her boss. If that didn't get her fired, then I would be surprised.

"Have you made contact with Honey yet?" I asked him when I wasdone and he shook his head.

"She's still been gone with Law. They haven't been back for days now," he said.

180

"Well, they should be back soon because he texted to say he wanted to see the kids soon," I informed him.

"You know what I don't understand?" he said and I looked up at him.

"What?" I asked and folded my arms.

"Why Law wasn't with you in the first place for Honey to even get with him? I mean it's no secret she left my ass for cheating. But judging by the hoops you're willing to jump through to get Law, I'm gonna assume that he left you," he said with a smirk on his face.

"Does it matter?" I asked and he ran his hand over his mouth.

"Yeah it does. Because if Law wasn't with your ass in the first place, breaking them up ain't gonna do shit because he still isn't going to be with your ass," he said laughing.

I shouldn't even be angry because he wasn't saying anything that was a lie. I had known Law nine years before Honey came on to the scene and he still didn't want my ass.

But in all honesty, I just didn't want him loving her.

"Of course we were together, I have his kids!" I lied.

"Ma, with all due respect, I don't know you and I've been fucking you raw for days now. It wouldn't surprise me if your ass got pregnant off of that. So please spare me with that

181

talk because I've got five baby mommas and I wasn't with none of them," he said, flaming up another blunt.

"Yeah well, think what you want; because if that was true, Law would have had more kids with other women. And in case your ass forgot, I'm the only bitch in town with his kids!" I rolled my eyes at him and he shook his head.

As I left his house, I was still fuming at what he said. But I knew that I was right about being the only bitch in town with Law's kids and I needed to break up him and Honey before she changed that fact!

Feeling pleased with the stunt I pulled earlier, I decided to go treat myself at the mall. The kids were with my grandma, so I was free.

I couldn't decide on what to do or get, so I stopped for some food at Popeye's. I was busy placing my order when someone caught my eye walking past the window outside.

I didn't even finish ordering; I just cut out of the line and ran after her. I almost broke my neck just to catch up to her but it was important. I needed to see if I saw what I thought I did.

And sure enough, she turned and confirmed what I knew I saw…a baby bump!

I didn't know Angel, but the only nigga I ever knew her to fuck was Law. Whenever I used to go to the club, he was in the back with her and only one thing happened in the back with him and that was fucking.

I also knew from hearing her talking about him, that he went in raw a few times here and there.

I tried to lie to myself hoping it would make me feel better but I knew in my heart that she was pregnant for him. I was so sure and proud that I was the only bitch in town with his kids but once again another bitch shitted on my parade.

"Yes, Monae, can I help you?" she looked at me.

"Angel, are you pregnant?" I asked and she laughed.

"Yep and before you ask, yes it's Law's baby. I ain't fucked anyone else but him the whole year," she smiled and my heart crushed into pieces.

Here I was, hoping that me having his kids would make him finally pick me once Honey was out of the way; but here came Angel pregnant.

"Does he know?" I asked and she nodded.

"Yep, and I told him that he better tell his bitch to make room," she said. "Anyway, I would love to talk but I have somewhere to be. Tell your kids they have a brother or sister on the way," she smiled and walked away.

183

Why was God punishing me? All I wanted was to have the man of my dreams all to myself, after stealing his seeds and getting pregnant for him. What was wrong with that?

I was crushed, but I wasn't at the same time, because I knew Angel being pregnant would definitely make Honey run for the hills now. I was bothered about Angel, but I wasn't at the same time, she was no real threat to me. Although Law fucked her, he never loved her. He never treated her any different from me. She didn't know where he lived; he never took her out or kissed her. The only time I saw him kiss her cheek was after her uncle died but never again after that.

I didn't need to worry about her too much. I had two kids for Law and it didn't change shit, so I knew her having his baby wouldn't change anything either.

I smiled because maybe Angel was exactly what I needed. All I needed to do was sit back and watch Honey fall apart because ofher.

Even if Law started fucking Angel again, it didn't matter because he would never make her his. And that left room for me once again!

I smiled as I made my way back to Popeye's. Angel was going to be a major part of my plan and she didn't even know it!

I'm cutting this chapter short because I'm about to be on some good bullshit. Operations 'bye, bye Honey' and 'cry me a motherfucking river bitch' was now in full swing.

*Hehehe*

## Chapter Thirteen

*Law*

It's been a week since my uncle revealed that he was Honey's dad and I had to tell her about Angel being pregnant.

My baby was having a hard time with life and it hurt knowing it was because of me. But I loved her and I didn't want to be with anyone else but her.

She didn't say much after I told her. She just sat quietly staring out of the window. Even though it was my fault for slipping up and fucking Angel raw a few times, I knew deep down she came out about the pregnancy because she saw me with Honey. The whole time she did nothing but call Honey all kinds of bitches, and I wanted to choke that hoe.

Honey was broken down and defeated. Life was turning upside down through no fault of her own. Maybe I should have set her free at that moment, but my heart wouldn't allow me to. My future was slipping through my fingers and I didn't know what to do.

Honey silently walked into the house and went straight to our room. I followed behind her with so much to say but I just couldn't talk. She emptied her duffle bag and

186

headed for the shower. She locked the door behind her and cut the shower on.

A nigga like me almost cried tears when I heard her crying in the shower, and it was a cry of pain.

Angel was on some next bullshit. Demanding me to tell Honey, demanding I attend all her appointments and demanding that she didn't want Honey involved

at all. She was worse than Monae. She kept constantly blowing up my phone for dumb shit like feeling sick. Bitch that's motherfucking morning sickness, the fuck can I do about it!

You would think this bitch was due any minute the way she was laying it on thick with shit hurting.

Motherfucking texting me telling me she needed all kinds of fucking food during the night. She was out of her goddamn mind.

I could have easily told her to dead that shit but after my pops died I promised no more death in my family if I could help it. And although Angel's ass meant nothing to me, she was indeed carrying my seed, my family.

Honey came out of the bathroom and her eyes were all red and swollen from crying, she could barely open them. She silently walked around to her side of the bed and climbed in. She pulled the blanket up close to her face and curled in a ball.

"What should I do, Honey?" I whispered.

"There's nothing you can do, Ky-mani," she sniffled.

"Do you want me to tell her to have an abortion, because I can't do that, Honey. I wish she wasn't pregnant but she is," I said, rubbing my hand all over my face in frustration.

"No, Ky-mani," she said, sitting up to look at me.

"You didn't do anything wrong. That was before my time and I have to accept it. But that doesn't mean it doesn't hurt Ky-mani. I'm only human, I don't know how to pretend that it's ok that another woman is carrying the child of the man I love," she said crying again.

"Do you want to end things with me?" I asked and she wiped her eyes.

"Do you?" she asked.

"No way, Honey. Ma, don't you understand how much I love you?" I said and she started crying again.

"I love you too, Ky-mani. I'm sorry, I will be ok. I don't want us to break up. I just need a little time," she said and I held her in my arms.

"Take all the time you need Honey but don't shut me out baby, please I beg you," I said and she nodded.

I held her in my arms until she cried herself to sleep. I was glad that she didn't want to end things but at the same time, I worried about if she could really handle Angel

188

having my baby?

I climbed out of the bed gently so I wouldn't wake her.

I needed to talk to my momma. I needed a voice of reason. I also texted Ricky and told him to come over.

"Momma?" I said into my cell.

"Baby, how you doing? How's Honey doing? Uncle Marco is going out of his mind. I had no idea he was her father," my momma said quietly so that let me know that they were still there.

"Honey is still in shock, to say the least. But I had to give her a blow of my own, Ma," I said and she went quiet.

"What you mean, Ky-mani?" she asked.

"Ma, do you remember that Jamaican girl I was seeing before I met Honey?"

"Yes. Oh God please don't tell me she's pregnant, Ky-mani," she said and I sighed.

"Yeah, momma she is."

"Oh Lord, Ky-mani no," she breathed out. "What did Honey say?" She asked.

"Ma, she has not stopped crying since I told her," I confessed feeling like shit.

"And Angel is on some bullshit. Talking about she doesn't want Honey involved and she's calling all hours talking shit," I moaned.

"Ky-mani, I don't know what to say, son. Does Honey

189

want to break up?"

"She said no but I'm just thinking how long will she feel like that with both Angel and Monae at her head?"

"Son, I know Honey loves you and I also know that you would never find anyone like her again. But as a woman who would have died if someone was pregnant for your daddy, I'm telling you that she might walk away because it hurts. But I hope she doesn't," she said and I dropped my head.

I sat and spoke with my momma a little more before Ricky arrived.

When he came in, he had a bottle of Hennessy with him. I chuckled when I saw it and dapped him up.

"Yo, my nigga, it's been a crazy few days for real," I said, pouring myself a cup and rolling up a blunt.

"I know, Cam called to tell me. So, does that make Honey my sister?" he asked and I laughed at him.

"I guess so," I shrugged my shoulder.

"Well, in that case, motherfucker I don't give you permission to fuck my sister," he said and I laughed my ass off.

"Nigga, I'm dead ass serious," he laughed. "But don't that make her yo' cousin?" he laughed and I held my middle finger up.

"Motherfucker ain't no blood between her and I so fuck that. I already dipped my dick in her, so fuck it. That's my

190

wife. Not even Unc can change that shit," I said and he laughed at me.

"Yo, sis must have that killer pussy, my nigga," he laughed hard.

"Nigga you don't know. I would murder the whole fucking world over her," I said dead ass serious and he laughed.

My phone started going off and when I looked it was messages from Angel.

*Angel: Law I'm the one motherfucking pregnant for you, not her ass! You need to come to me and see to me.*

*Angel: Law my whole-body hurts, can't you come over. Tell Honey to take a seat!!!*

*Angel: Law I feel so sick, please come over.*

*Angel: Law don't ignore me!*

This bitch went on and on and on. "One minute, my nigga," I told Ricky before I ran upstairs to check on Honey. She was still sound asleep. I tiptoed to my closet and grabbed my nine from the safe. I tucked it in my waist and left the room quietly.

"Take a ride with me, Cuz," I said, grabbing my phone and keys from the center table.

191

I jumped in my all black Range and sped off towards Angel. She wanted me to come, and my ass was going over.

"I'mma be a minute, ok?" I said and Ricky nodded and rolled down the window so his ass could hear. I shook my head laughing at him and climbed out the truck.

I made two taps on Angel's door with my nine and when she saw it as she opened the door, she tried to close it back but I grabbed her.

"What's wrong, Angel? You wanted me here, so I'm here," I said, putting the gun under her chin.

"Law, I...I..." she stuttered.

"What, Angel?" I said and she started shaking.

"This is the first and last time I'm telling yo' ass this; so listen to me good," I said and she nodded.

"Don't ever call or text my phone ever fucking again, bitch. Yo' ass is pregnant from a casual fuck, not because I want your ass. I would never ever leave my queen for your motherfucking ass! Never!!! I ain't your man, bitch, so don't get shit twisted. You will respect my woman and keep your ass in your thot lane and learn your role, bitch!" I shook her.

"Unless that baby is coming out of your pussy, don't call my motherfucking phone. When I'm at home with my queen don't you think about texting my phone because if you upset,

Honey, I will murder your fucking ass, Angel. Don't play me," I gritted my teeth.

"You're really willing to kill for her?" she asked as tears streamed down her face.

"You bet your ass. I would kill every motherfucker in town over my baby. Her pussy is life, remember I told you that," I said, releasing her.

I put my gun back on my waist and walked back to my car. As usual, Ricky was killing himself laughing.

"Damn, Cuz, you got a bitch shook," he laughed.

"Good. Fucking side piece thot wanna catch wifey status because her ass is pregnant. Fuck outta here. Her ass is just a vessel for my seed," I said loud enough for to hear as she was still standing by the door looking at me.

She closed the door with her head down and I drove back to my house. Some may call it drastic but Honey was already having a hard time dealing with the fact that Angel was pregnant. I didn't need Angel making shit worse. She knew exactly what she was doing. Calling and texting me knowing I was in the house with Honey. She was trying to cause trouble and I had to shut that shit down. And I needed her to know I wasn't playing!

# Chapter Fourteen

*Honey*

I cried so fucking much, my whole body hurt. These last few weeks were some goddamn trying times. I cried so much I could have filled Lake Michigan ten times over. Cry me a river wasn't shit compared to the amount of crying I did. I was surprised Ky-mani didn't put my ass in a mental hospital.

I couldn't help it, though. When he told me that Angel was pregnant, my soul ached. I knew it happened before he met me and I should have been glad it didn't happen through him cheating or anything, but it was more about the fact that the only two men I had ever loved had kids and none were from me.

Mani and Chyna were growing kids already when I met Ky-mani so it didn't bother me too much, but Angel was physically still carrying his child. That was a sentimental moment between two people; something so sacred and

194

special, a bond between them that I never had.

I could see it worried Ky-mani but I tried my best to reassure him that I was okay with it. I didn't want to break up with him, so I swallowed it up as much as I could and I was going to roll with it. If I can love Chyna and Mani, then I could love this baby too. I know Angel was giving him a rough time because of me but as long as Ky-mani fought for us, I was going to stand by him.

If we could overcome almost getting kidnapped; then we could overcome this together.

Oh, and let's not forget Marco's confession. I guess all his staring and ignoring me made sense. Not only did he reveal he's my father, but Cameron is now also my brother; and Ricky too. I kept asking God for a bigger family, and I guess he answered my ass.

Marco was still trying to reach out to me; I did understand why he left. I always wondered how I got that scar on my back but my momma always told me I fell playing. I should have given him a chance to explain but a part of me felt like I was betraying my momma talking to him. I decided to call my momma; I think it was time that she knew.

"Hey, my baby, how you doing?" she said when she

answered.

I wish I could have told her about me almost getting kidnapped, but I could never tell her about Ky-mani being Law, so "good momma," is what I said.

"How's Ky-mani doing? Work? Everything ok? You still living with him?" she asked a million questions but I couldn't think straight. My lips were itching to tell her about Marco.

"Momma fine. Everything and Ky-mani is fine. I actually called you momma because I met someone," I said and she went silent.

"What do you mean you met someone? Honey, are you leaving Ky-mani or cheating on him?" she asked angrily.

One thing about the females in my family, we didn't play that hoe card with cheating and shit. At all times, we acted like ladies. My momma always told me to walk away when a nigga wrongs you, so you keep your dignity, but never because you met another man and want him instead.

"Momma, no never. I love Ky-mani. He makes me happy," I told her and she sighed.

"But I meant I met someone you know," I said and she laughed.

"Oh yeah. Was it Carol? She said she saw you a few weeks ago," she said laughing.

"No, Momma."

"Oh someone I went to school with?"

"I don't think you did," I said.

"Oh right. I can't think of who then Honey. Do you know their name?" she asked and I went silent.

"Um yeah, I know his name," I cleared my throat. "It's Marco Ramsey," I said and the line went silent.

"Honey, what did you just say!?!" she asked and I repeated the name.

"Oh god," she said.

"Honey, baby, how?" she asked me.

"He's Ky-mani's step-uncle. So, is he telling the truth? Is he my daddy, momma?" I asked and she sighed heavily.

"Yes, Honey, he's your father," she said silently.

I couldn't help it; the tears started flowing once again. "Baby, please don't cry," she said and I wiped my eyes.

"Momma, what happened? Why didn't you ever talk about him or tell me his name?"

"Because Honey, I was angry that he left us and for your protection, I didn't want you to try to find him or speak his name and people figured it out. I didn't want to tell you it was somebody else and then you look for that person so it was best if I never told you," she said.

"He's not a bad man, Honey. He was so good to us, to you especially. He loved you so much. But his lifestyle

197

wouldn't allow us to be together as a family. Whenever trouble came, they came after you, Honey, to get to him. We always got away but the last time was the worst. They almost killed him and you. You were in the hospital for weeks; doctors thought that you would never walk again. He walked away to protect us and he made me promise to keep you away," she said and I cried even harder.

"I'm sorry, my baby, I really am. But I guess you were supposed to meet Ky-mani because meeting him made you find Marco. How is he doing? Did you meet your brother, Cameron, too? He was just a little boy when I met your father," she said.

"Marco is doing fine momma. He lives near River North with Ky-mani's aunt Ruth. And yeah, I met Cameron but I have another brother named Ricky; he's aunt Ruth's son. Can you believe that momma, I have two brothers," I laughed and so did she.

"Oh, Honey really? That's so good baby. I always felt bad leaving you without a family in Chicago but I wanted you to live your dream. And I'm glad you did because now you have a father and two brothers. Don't hate him for what he had to do, Honey. Talk to him and get to know him. Know that I love you, baby, and I support you and want you to get to know him ok?" she said and I smiled.

We spoke some more on the phone and she made me promise that I would try and talk to him. Speaking to my momma made me realize that it was out of love that he left me and nothing else. The fact he kept that picture in his wallet after all these years let me know it too. But I needed to get over the initial hurt and surprise. Although I cried, I felt much better after talking to my momma.

Once I finished work today, I was going to ask Ky-mani to bring me to see Marco.

I quickly washed my face again and showered for work. Ky-mani left out earlier to see to the new house. I sent him a quick text and went off to work.

I strolled off into my building feeling somewhat happy but that didn't last. I was immediately yoked up and brought into my manager's office.

"Miss Sinclair, is something wrong?" I asked as I sat down at her desk.

"I don't know, Honey, you tell me," she said, handing me a piece of paper.

My eyes bucked out of my head when I read what she handed me. It was an email from my personal account calling my manager all kinds of bitches and hoes but that wasn't it. She also handed me emails from huge clients who informed her that I had sent them emails asking them to leave my firm because of my thieving stank ass bitch of a manager.

"Miss Sinclair, I never sent those emails. I swear to God I never sent them emails," I pleaded but it fell on deaf eyes.

"Isn't that your email address?" she asked.

I looked over the address and it was mine alright.

"Yes, it is but I didn't send them. Please, Miss Sinclair."

"I'm sorry, Honey. But those emails were passed to the board. They've already dismissed you, Honey," she said and a single tear came from my eyes.

"I have no choice but to have you escorted off the premises," she said and just as the words left her mouth, two security guards walked in.

"You have ten minutes to collect your items," she said, looking at me over her designer glasses.

I wiped my face, stood to my feet, and walked out with my head up. I could see my girls standing by looking at me. They wanted to approach me but I wouldn't allow them. I didn't want them in trouble on my account. I quickly grabbed my belongings and walked out of my dream job.

I cried like a damn baby all the way home. I thought about calling or texting Ky-mani but I didn't want to stress him. So, I decided to tell him later once he got home. I was supposed to have a quick drink with the girls after work so he had planned to hang with his boys for a while before coming home. I didn't want to spoil that, so I decided I would lie in bed and read my kindle until later.

I changed into a night shirt, put my headphones in and indulged myself in a book to occupy my mind. I loved my job more than anything and if I sat thinking about what happened, I knew it would break me. So, reading was the only way I wouldn't think too much.

I decided to read *Thug Passion* by Mz Lady P since it had the most parts to it and it came highly recommended by Tasha.

It was a good idea because a few hours and a few books later, I had calmed down a whole lot. I sat and thought about what I could make for dinner and then my phone rang.

"What's up, bitch?" I said to Tasha.

"Honey, are you ok?" she asked.

"I'm ok, Tasha. I don't know who sent those emails but it wasn't me," I said.

"I'm sorry about that," she said. "Um, where are you?" she asked.

"I'm home why?"

"Is Ky-mani there?"

"No, he's with his boys? Why is something wrong? Did something happen to him?" I started to panic.

"No, Honey! Nothing happened. It's just," she said but stopped.

"It's just what, Tasha?"

"Have you been on Facebook today?" she asked, causing me to grab my iPad.

"No, I've been reading. Did your stupid ass tag me in something again?" I asked, laughing but when she didn't I knew something was up.

"No, Honey. Look you're gonna see it anyway. But Monae put something up on Facebook and tagged you," she finally spat it out.

"Tagged me? What you mean she tagged me, for what?" I said, logging into my Facebook.

And then my question was answered. Right there on my page for the whole world to see was a picture of Ky-mani lying shirtless and pant less with his arm around Monae. She captioned the photo '***when your baby daddy comes to see the kids but falls into your pussy instead***' and tagged me.

She was lying naked next to him and he was out cold which he always did after sex.

But that pic wasn't as bad as the next. This bitch took a pic of her mouth around his dick. His eyes were closed and his hands were back over his head. The next photo Facebook deleted so I could only imagine it must have been a pic of them fucking.

"Honey, are you there?" I heard Tasha's voice. I was so engrossed in what I just saw that I completely forget she was on the phone.

"Honey?" she called me again.

"Yeah I'm here. I um, I gotta go, Tasha. Sorry," I said and hung up.

My hands were shaking and my stomach felt sick as I looked at the pics again. My heart was racing and my head was spinning. The comments started filling my wall and I had notification after notification as Facebook world erupted with chatter over these pictures.

I then started receiving text messages and tweet notifications.

My phone started ringing and it was the rest of the girls, Ky-mani's momma, and sisters, and an unknown number who I assumed was Marco.

"I've had enough!" I screamed out in frustration.

First, my apartment and car were set on fire, then my ass nearly gets kidnapped, then I find my father on the same night my boyfriend tells me he got another woman pregnant; I lose my job, and now my boyfriend cheats on me and his bitch posts it on Facebook!

I couldn't take any more. I was physically and emotionally drained. My body just couldn't take any more.

*I can't do this anymore.* I thought.

I looked around me and I didn't know what the hell to do. Should I sit around and wait for Ky-mani to eventually stop fucking Monae and come home to explain to me or do I just say fuck it and leave?

I jumped out of bed and grabbed my suitcase. Yeah, I chose fuck it.

I pulled on leggings and a t-shirt before packing up most of my clothes and shoes into suitcases. When I grabbed everything I wanted and needed, I turned out the lights and walked out.

My phone kept on ringing, so I cut that shit off as I climbed into my truck. I could feel the tears trying to form but I blinked those suckers away. I had done more crying in the last month than I've done my whole fucking life and I was done with it. I wasn't going to allow another tear to fall from my eyes.

I started my truck and drive off fast into the night. I know it was risky going near River North since his family lived there, but it was where I was raised so it was all I knew.

I booked myself a room at the Marriott Hotel that sat right on the border of another town. I wasn't stupid; I took cash from home and paid for two weeks.

I wasn't about to have Ky-mani trace my fucking credit card.

Fuck that nigga.

After a hot bath, I pulled on some pajamas, pulled the blanket up over my head and went right to sleep.

As far as I was concerned that could have each other!

I was done!

# Chapter Fifteen

*Law*

Honey was still down about Angel but she was trying. I could see that she was having a hard time but I knew that she loved me. We were able to talk and laugh still, but whenever something came up about Angel or reminded her about the pregnancy, she would shell up and go quiet.

I couldn't do anything but apologize to her. The only good thing was that after my little talk, Angel was no longer calling or texting me.

Marco was trying his hardest to get Honey to talk to him, but I told him to give her some more time. She didn't even talk to me about it so I wanted to wait until she was ready to.

Can you believe the whole time I was with Unc, I was around my girl's dad and didn't even know!

After a quick morning and afternoon by the club and restaurant, I called my boys to meet up, since Honey was meeting the girls after work for a while. She told me she spoke to her mom and finally was ready to talk to Marco. I was happy that she did because Marco really wasn't a bad man; and being from the streets myself and facing issues with niggas gunning for me, I could completely see why he chose to stay away from Honey.

"What's up, my niggas?" I smiled and yelled as I approached them.

"What's up, Law?" they all rang out one by one.

"Ayo, Cuz, let me holler at you for a minute; it's really important too," Cam said walking over to me. He dapped me first and then adjusted his fitted snapback.

"Aye, you ok, Cameron?" I asked because he looked serious as fuck.

"Um, I just wanted to say…" he started and was shuffling on his feet. "Motherfucker, you ain't allowed to fuck my sister, nigga!" he yelled and busted out laughing with everyone else.

Ricky ran over and gave him a stupid ass handshake as they continued to laugh.

"Niggas, fuck y'all," I laughed. "In fact, I don't give my woman permission to be y'all crazy ass fuckers' sister. The fuck you mean!" I spat and they were laughing so hard at me.

"Shit, she was my woman before she was y'all sister," I folded my arms and sucked my teeth. "For that, I'mma make sure I slide my dick all the way up your sister tonight especially," I said.

"Alright, my nigga, but you forgetting one thing," Cam said and I tilted my head at him as to say what.

"You're just fucking a female version of me, my nigga. That's my blood flowing through her veins," Cameron said and looked at me.

I stopped laughing for a second and stared him down. His lips were shaking because he was fighting so hard not to laugh. Ricky, however, didn't give a shit and was bending over laughing his ass off.

"Nigga, what the fuck ever! She don't be looking like your ugly ass anyway!" I said and he fell out laughing and dapped me up.

"Y'all motherfuckers leave my ass alone with that sister shit. My name is written in that pussy. I don't give a fuck who she related to – fuck with me. I'll fuck her and send y'all a voice note with her screaming my name, y'all keep fucking with me," I said and we all laughed.

"Nah fuck that. We good. It's bad even knowing you infecting our sister with your crazy ass but don't nobody wanna hear that shit," Cam said, shaking his head.

We laughed and kicked it for a while. I kept checking my phone to see if Honey texted to say she was done with the girls but she hadn't yet. So, I thought I would chill for a little while longer and then head home.

My phone rang and I huffed when I saw that it was Monae.

"Yes, Monae," I answered with an attitude.

"Daddy," I heard and realized that it was Chyna.

"Hey, baby, what's wrong?"

"I can't sleep, daddy. There's a monster in my room under my bed and it won't go away. Could you get it please, Daddy?" she said, sounding like she wanted to cry. My kids were my heart and I loved them to the moon and back.

I was about ready to go home anyway, so I could easily stop by and get the monster for Chyna and then head home in time to meet Honey.

"Sure, baby, I'm going to come right now," I said and she happily accepted. I quickly dapped it up with my niggas and headed out to Monae's crib.

"Hey, Monae," I said when she opened the door.

"Hi, Law," she smiled at me.

I didn't even bother saying anything else to her, I just stepped pass and went to Chyna's bedroom.

She was sitting up in bed with dried tears on her face when I walked in. "Oh, the monster got daddy's baby scared?" I said, picking her up and hugging her.

"Show me, baby," I told her, putting her down on the

floor and dropping to my knees.

"Under there," she pointed and I laughed.

"Ok, monster. I'm Chyna's dad and I said you gotta get up outta here before I kick your butt," I said to nothing.

"Yeah! My daddy said leave," she said, sounding like a little thug and I laughed.

"So Na Na, is it gone?" I asked and she nodded.

"But Daddy you have to lay down with me so it won't come back," she said with her hand on her hips.

I looked at the clock on her wall and saw that it wasn't that late. So, I could spare another ten minutes or so with her.

Because I had been out all day drinking and smoking with the boys, I decided to take my clothes off before getting in the bed with her. I stripped down to my boxers alone and laid on top of her blanket with her under it.

I placed an arm around her and rocked her gently to sleep....

I felt a warm sensation around my dick and it stirred me from my sleep. Honey had never sucked my dick before but I liked it. I pulled my arms above my head and moaned. My baby had my ass feeling good like I wanted to nut already. But then I remembered something important...I

210

wasn't home!

I quickly opened my eyes and when I did, I saw Monae about to sit on my dick. I pushed that bitch real hard and she fell face first to the floor. I jumped up off the bed and put my dick away.

I looked around the room but realized Chyna was no longer in the room.

"Bitch, what the fuck you think you doing? You tryna take dick in my motherfucking daughter's bed! Are you fucking nuts?!?!" I grunted at her.

"Well, we can go into my room then," she said, reaching for me but I pushed her hand away.

"Bitch, my dick will never ever touch your pussy again. One, I would never in my life cheat on Honey with you! And two, even if you were the last bitch on earth I still wouldn't fuck you. I would rather cut my own dick off," I growled and grabbed my clothes.

Nasty, trifling bitch. She really wanted to fuck in a child's bed, in *my* child's bed? And she was trying to ride me raw, the bitch was fucking crazy.

She stood and watched me as I pulled on my clothes. I

211

made sure my phone and keys were in there before I rushed out of the room.

I peeked my head into Mani's room and saw that Chyna was in there too and they were both fast asleep.

I hurried down the stairs and rushed to the door with Monae right behind me. But when I pulled on the door it didn't open. The bitch locked me in.

"Open the door, Monae," I turned and said to her.

"No! Give me what I want and I will open it," she said.

"Monae, open the fucking door!" I yelled but she shook her head.

"Just one fuck Law and I will open the door," she said.

"Monae, I'm going to ask one more time, open the door. Now!" I warned her but instead she dropped her robe revealing her naked body.

And I lost my fucking cool.

I grabbed her by her throat and lifted her off the ground. She slapped my hands, choking and kicking her feet.

"Or how about I kill your ass right here right now and take the keys from your dead body," I said in her face.

I squeezed her neck until her eyes rolled back and then I

let go, dropping her to the floor.

She coughed and choked trying to catch her breath. I looked around for the keys but couldn't find it. So I went to grab her again and she held her hand up.

"Ok. Ok. They're in my shoes by the door," she whispered and coughed.

I walked over to her shoes and found them. I took them out and unlocked the door, and walked out. When I looked at the time it was two hours later. I can't believe I fell asleep putting Chyna to bed.

I grabbed my phone out of my pocket and for the first time realized I had over thirty missed calls and just as many texts messages. The bitch had put my phone on silent.

I saw that I had a lot of calls from Ricky, my momma, and both of my sisters. I instantly thought something was up. Before I could read through my text messages, Ricky was calling me back.

"Yo, fam, where the fuck are you?" he said.

"I'm about to go home. What's wrong?" I asked.

"Oh, nigga you by Monae's. Shit," he said.

"Yeah," I said and then I heard my call-waiting beeping in my ear and looked to see it was my momma.

"Yo, G, it's my momma let me call you right back," I

213

said.

"Nigga, it's on Facebook!" I heard him yell as I switched the call to my momma.

"Hey, Momma, you alright?"

"Ky-mani, what the fuck is wrong with your no behaving ass! How could you do Honey like that, Ky-mani, really?!!" She yelled.

"Momma, what are you talking about?"

"Nigga, don't what you talking about momma, me. The whole fucking town knows you're at Monae's house cheating on Honey. It's all over motherfucking Facebook. Your sisters and I been calling Honey but she isn't answering. How could you fuck up so badly for Monae?" she said.

Am I missing something?

"Momma, you know damn well I didn't fuck Monae. Now, what's all this talk about fucking Facebook and everybody knowing I cheated on Honey?" I asked.

My momma sucked her teeth. "Nigga, go and check Honey's Facebook and if that girl leaves your ass, that's your own damn fault," she barked before hanging up in my face.

I was confused. I caught Monae trying to fuck me, so how the hell does my whole family know that shit and why does my momma actually believe that I did it.

I opened the Facebook app on my phone and found Honey's page and then I saw it.

My dick in Monae's mouth all over fucking Facebook. This bitch had taken pics of her and I lying in my daughter's bed with her ass butt naked. One of the pics was deleted but after going through all my text messages, my momma had texted the deleted pic to my phone. And it was one with Monae about to sit her pussy on my dick!

And I knew for sure that if the whole town saw it, so did Honey! I grabbed my nine from my glove compartment and rushed to Monae's door. I didn't even knock; I just kicked that motherfucker in.

I ran up the stairs and found her lying in her bed. I jumped on the bed, shoes and all and grabbed her by the hair lifting her up off the bed. I put my nine under her chin and put my finger on the trigger.

"No, Law, please I'm sorry," she cried.

"You sorry! You got my dick on Facebook, you got the whole fucking town and my family thinking that I fucked you and cheated on Honey, and you sorry?! Bitch you tagged my woman in those pics!" I screamed in her face.

"I finally found someone who truly loves me and instead of being happy for me, you've made it your mission to

215

fuck things up!"

"But I love you, Law."

"YOU DON'T LOVE ME! You love my dick and money because if I didn't have that, your ass wouldn't even want me! I should kill your ass right fucking now. You fucking thot. I fucking hate your ass, Monae," I pushed the gun deeper into her chin. My finger was itching to pull the trigger.

I looked on her bed and saw her laptop.

"Please don't, Law, I'm sorry," she said with tears seeping down her face.

"Get your laptop and you're going to write every fucking word I tell you to and if you don't, I'm going to beat your ass," I said, slapping her across the face. I'm not a nigga who beats women but she needed that. Monae constantly thought I was playing with her but not this time.

She grabbed her cheek and cried harder.

"Shut your ass up! Were you crying when you were doing the shit and tagging Honey?" I said and she shut up.

"First of all take that motherfucking post down now and delete those pics. Got my momma seeing my dick and shit! Damn, bitch!" I spat.

She nodded her head when it was down.

"Now type this word for word," I said, standing over her aiming my gun.

"I'm a lying little bitch who likes to lie on my pussy. Law never fucked me, he fell asleep putting our daughter to bed. So, I took my nasty thot pussy self into the room he was in and took those photos as he slept. We didn't fuck, I said that because I can't handle the fact that he never wanted my hoe ass so my no- good ass is trying to break him up with his woman. He hates my sneaky pussy self and would never fuck me even if I was the last woman on earth. I'm just a sad, pathetic, lonely, desperate bitch, and I'm sorry, Honey," I said and she typed away.

"Show me," I told her and she did.

"Now post it and leave it up there," I told her.

I grabbed her again and slammed her into the wall.

"Monae, for your own safety stop fucking with me. If we have to have this conversation again, you won't like it. Understand?" I said and she nodded her head.

"I hope for your sake that Honey hasn't left me because I feel sorry for you if she has," I said and she started shaking.

I let her go and walked out. As I raced home in my car, I called Honey's cell over and over but it was off. And she never turns her phone off.

When I got home, I didn't see her car outside and I

feared the worst.

As soon as I parked the car, I took off running into the house. All the lights were off.

"Honey!" I called over and over again as I frantically searched each room, but when I walked into our room, I knew she was gone.

The opened empty drawers and empty hangers in the closet confirmed what I already knew…my baby was gone!

## Chapter Sixteen

*Monae*

I had to do what I did to Law, but I didn't think it would've ended that way. I planned all day what I would do and coached Chyna on what to say. Well, I beat her ass to make sure she did it. Don't judge me; I was in love with Law. I knew we would be good together if he just allowed it.

I mean he came over instantly when Chyna called him. And the way he tended to her and did all that he did to calm her and put her to bed, how could I not love a man like that?

He made me wet just hearing him talk to her so lovingly. When I locked the door after he came in, it all played out differently in my mind. Yes, posting it was risky, but if he did fuck me I wouldn't have been lying; and if I didn't post them, how was I supposed to let her know?

Sure, I could have easily texted her alone, but I wanted to

humiliate her the way she did me that night at his birthday. Up until recently, people still made remarks about it to me and on my page. I had people tag me in pictures of her and him on that night. I wanted her to feel how I felt that night.

And with the whole town knowing, I knew that she would be more likely to leave him.

And let's not forget about that video circling of her punching my ass! This bitch had me on my ass looking pathetic!!! I had to do something back.

Once he was inside her room, all I had to do was wait until he fell asleep. When he did, I could hardly contain myself. I quickly grabbed Chyna and put her in Mani's bed.

When I went back into that room with him sprawled out over her bed, my mouth watered something hard. He was so damn fine. His skin looked so smooth and sexy. The tattoos made my pussy jump. His impressive dick that I could see through his briefs had me so wet.

Why couldn't he just be mine? Why shouldn't he be mine?

I grabbed my phone, took off my clothes and climbed in bed. I laid on his arm and he automatically put it around me. Damn it felt so good. I snapped a few pics like that and posted it right away. And then my eyes looked down at his dick.

My mouth and pussy were dying to taste it like I was dying of hungry and thirst.

I slid down onto my knees, released his dick and put it in my mouth, and after a few seconds, that shit started to grow in my mouth. I quickly snapped more pics as it hardened and posted them. Then he started moving his hips up into my mouth, and I snapped those pics too. The moaning started and he grabbed my head pushing me further and yep I snapped those pics too.

I didn't care that he moaned her bitch ass name. Once he felt this pussy again, he would be moaning my name. I quickly let go and straddled over him. And just as I grabbed his dick and snapped a pic of me sliding down on it, he woke up and pushed me off.

I literally landed on the floor; face first and my pussy in the air. He had never pushed me like that.

When he raced down the stairs and found the door locked, I thought for sure he would fuck me just like before when I used to corner him in his office. He used to end up doing it anyway. But he didn't. Even when I grabbed onto his leg and begged him, he told me no.

She must really have a hold on him because no matter what, he wouldn't fuck me.

When he grabbed me by the throat and squeezed the way he did, I knew I had pushed him. Even though I wanted him to do that, but with his dick deep inside me. What! I love that man!!

But when he squeezed tighter and tighter and I felt myself losing strength, I knew at that point that he would gladly choke my ass out over her. I had no choice but to let him out.

221

When he left, I cried my heart out. If only he would love me like that.

He wasn't cheating on Honey for anything; I saw his eyes and he meant that shit.

He was actually scared of losing her. And if for a second I doubted that, he educated my ass when he kicked my door down and pushed a gun in my face.

I had never been so scared in my life. His eyes changed and he looked out of his mind. The fear I felt from him over her was too real; like he would literally die without her. He had never hit me before, so when he did, it hurt more than the slap itself.

I didn't want to write what he told me to, because honestly, the people I knew wasn't shit. After I posted the pictures and tagged Honey, I expected comments laughing at her.

But instead, they called me desperate and jealous. They called me all kinds of bitches and wished that Law and Honey would beat my ass.

Then someone even went beyond and uploaded a pic of me and one of Honey and started a poll of who they thought Law would rather fuck out of the both of us.

I guess I don't need to say that they voted for Honey. They weren't even there and they knew I was lying; accusing me of drugging the man, like that was the only way he would fuck me.

So, I knew posting what he told me to would be the end of me. I didn't even press send good before comments started flooding in of people laughing and winning wagers about being right that Law wouldn't knowingly fuck me over a beauty like Honey.

Once he made me do that, I knew I would never ever again taste his dick.

My plans to have him and another baby were over.

I was so embarrassed; I cut my phone off and deleted my Facebook app. I could never show my face in public again after that and I didn't plan on to.

I knew Law was going to kill me one day.

Especially as I had sent a few pictures to Honey's cell phone.

But I wasn't done. I wouldn't be me if I was. I couldn't have him and that was fine, but I damn sure wasn't going to let him have her!

I would just have to continue with fucking her life up on the low and if that still didn't work…

Then the bitch will just have to die, won't she!

*To be continued*

Made in the USA
Columbia, SC
21 September 2017